ENCHANTED FOOTBALL

DENISE KAHN

978-0-9978231-5-8 (Paperback)
978-0-9978231-6-5 (E-Book)

Published by 4Agapi

Publisher's Cataloging-In-Publication Data
(Prepared by The Donohue Group, Inc.)

Names: Kahn, Denise, author.
Title: Enchanted football / Denise Kahn.
Description: [Albuquerque, New Mexico] : 4Agapi, [2019]
Identifiers: ISBN 9780997823158 (paperback) | ISBN
    9780997823165 (ebook)
Subjects: LCSH: Football teams--New Mexico--Fiction. |
    Professional athletes--New Mexico--Fiction. |
    Accidents--Fiction. | Teamwork (Sports)--Fiction. |
    LCGFT: Humorous fiction. | Sports fiction.
Classification: LCC PS3611.A43 E53 2019 (print) | LCC
    PS3611.A43 (ebook) | DDC 813/.6--dc23

DeniseKahnBooks.com / DeniseKahnVoices.com

Books by Denise Kahn

Novels
Peace of Music
Obsession of the Heart
Warrior Music
Music trilogy
Guitar Woman (Novella)
Split-Second Lifetime
Hot Air
Enchanted Football

Travel Tales
(Short travel stories)
We were 12 at 12:12 on 12/12/12 (Mexico)
Entertained by the Gods (Greece)
Sai Baba's Ashram Rendezvous (India)
Gstaad Grace (Switzerland)
Thanksgiving in 24 Hours (Mexico)
Olympic Honor (Italy)

Short Stories
Miraculous Moments;
True Stories Affirming that Life goes on,
By Elissa Al-Chokhachy

Photo Book
Around the World in 80 Quotes on Photos

Children's Series
Violet's Voyages:
Switzerland: The St. Bernard Adventure

Praise for Denise Kahn

Peace of Music

What a thrill this novel is, especially for me, since I am Greek and a singer and have lived in many of the places in the book. It portrays beautifully the history of my country, some of which I lived through. Most of all, I truly love the way music is intertwined in the story. Musicians will not be able to put this book down, nor anyone else who appreciates a good novel.
Nana Mouskouri, Opera and contemporary singer,
UNICEF Ambassador, Author

Music to Your Eyes. This magnificent work of literary art spans four continents and the lives of the unforgettable and colorful characters.
Jada Ryker, Bestselling Author

Obsession of the Heart

This tale is centred around a singing diva called Davina. From the first page the story whisks the reader along, from one crisis to another as we meet many other colourful characters along the way. This is very much an adventure story with love, deception and loyalty thrown into the mixture.
The pace is quick as the action travels from country to country in a world of super stardom, yet very real human emotions. Hold onto your seats in this roller coaster of a journey!
Sonya C. Dodd, Author

Warrior Music

Denise Kahn wrote a masterpiece directly imagined from her heart as her own son, a U.S. Marine was in Iraq in harm's way… My hat is off to the author and most respectfully to her son and to all that serve in the United States Military. A must read for anyone looking for a love story with non-stop action.
Marc A. DiGiacomo, Multi-award Bestselling Author,
Law Enforcement Officer

Just an incredible read for me and brought back memories of my 20 + years in the military. Most highly recommended with additional Hoo-Rahs and a Bravo Zulu to this author.
A Navy Vet/Amazon Top 500 Reviewer

It will soon be categorized as a historical novel because it superbly chronicles the life of a soldier in the desert of Iraq, post 9/11… Ms. Kahn's son is a veteran of the Iraq War, and this novel is her love song to him. Her pride of him and all veterans shines through in this novel of love, war, and music.
P.A. McAlister, Author

The Music Trilogy

This is an exquisite saga. A beautifully woven tale covering several generations of one family whose paths are intertwined with an amazing Chinese vase. Although the story begins in China, the plot covers a range of countries and continents as well as several centuries as the magic of the vase touches the lives of the family to whom it belongs. The writing is beautiful, the characters are rich and varied and the pace changes from the smooth to the rough of World War. Be prepared to lose yourself in an amazing world of music, laughter and intrigue as you follow the vase from thirteenth century China to modern day Europe.
This novel will not fail to capture the imagination of the reader.
Sonya C. Dodd, Author

Split-Second Lifetime

This book will become a classic! Isabel Allende, Paulo Coelho, Denise Kahn. What do they have in common? They are all amazing writers and storytellers with a touch of mysticism. Ms. Kahn's writing is fluid and elegant. The characters are original and compassionate, the story is intriguing and fascinating, and the settings are international and exotic. Unique scenes will stay in the back of your mind for a long time. Each one of these authors has a specialty or unique ingredient that puts them in a class of their own.
Denise Kahn's 'Split-Second Lifetime', like 'House of Spirits' and 'the Alchemist', is bound to become a classic.
Racquel, Amazon Reviewer

A Beautiful Quilting of Sounds and Images. The author took on a panoramic project with her book and did a magnificent job. I learned more about other cultures and ways of thinking. At the same time, the writing style was lyrical, entertaining, and brought together images, sounds, flavors, and sensations. The book even encompasses humor. The entertaining and unexpected puns made me laugh out loud. Jada Ryker, Bestselling Author

Denise Kahn's writing is highly sensual. "Dodi's words were music to my ears and a symphony in my heart." Her work is further enriched by her exposure to different nations, as she describes details from foreign settings and cultures.
Uvi Posnansky, Bestselling Author

Guitar Woman

A novella full of passion that covers art, music and the sensuous side of human nature. The manner in which the reader is drawn into the sights, sounds and smells of Athens is indeed magical. The food at the tavern made my mouth water! The description of the uniforms of the select few guarding the Tomb of the Unknown Soldier are indeed memorable.
Serenity, Amazon Hall of Fame Top 10 Reviewer

Hot Air

This is my first ride with Ms. Kahn and it won't be my last... with a host of elegantly drawn characters in an array of beautifully described scenarios. Denise Kahn has a wonderful, comfortable writing style and her novel Hot Air is fun, exciting, informed and intelligently rendered.
Sean Costello, Bestselling Author

The story is powerful, as they are in all of Denise Kahn's books (this is not my first by this author, and definitely not last). Her characters come alive. The half Navajo half Irish hot air balloon pilot and elite Pararescueman, his Greek playboy buddy, the Canadian world skiers and the Afghan extremist are but some of the personalities that cross paths that will keep you on the edge of your seat.
Helen A., Amazon reader

Around the World in 80 Quotes on Photos

As I sit here in the frozen tundra of New England, I can say that I truly appreciated this photographic journey around the world, especially to warmer places! The quotes added a certain serenity to the experience, and I can honestly say the author has rekindled my desire to travel!
James Tredeau, Professor of French

Inspirational, beautiful and informative. Take 80 inspirational quotes that will get you thinking about a variety of life's greatest truths, The photos are as thought-provoking as the notable quotations - and add an element of beauty that only they can. If you wish to take an entertaining trip around the world without leaving your desk chair, this book will provide you with your round-trip ticket. I highly recommend this beautiful and stimulating book.
Dr. Joe Rubino, Center For Personal Reinvention

DEDICATION

To Football and Sports Aficionados,
Native Americans, and New Mexicans.

And of course for my own 'little' fans,
my son Michael, and all his buddies.

*I have seen that in any great undertaking it is not enough
for a man to depend simply upon himself.*
Shooter Teton Sioux

We will be know forever by the tracks we leave.
Dakota

CONTENTS

ENCHANTED FOOTBALL

DENISE KAHN

PROLOGUE

Neil Howard cringed in pain as two enormous linebackers from the opposing team tackled him. He wondered if any of his ribs were cracking as it wasn't just one sack, rather they were repetitive blows by massive hands delivering the agony. His mind was playing games as he faded in and out from the pain. He realized *he* was that quarterback on the field, 'one of the best the game has ever seen', he remembered an announcer saying about him. He looked at his surroundings. He wasn't moving rhythmically on the manicured grass ready to throw a perfect spiral to one of his wide receivers; no, Neil was in a dark, filthy alley getting the life beaten out of him. He wanted to cry, not because of the pain invading what seemed every inch of his body, but because he had become a bad caricature of someone who once was a brilliant quarterback—a leader of magnificent athletes, of professional football players who depended on him and looked up to him—until he discovered a new game and his eventual demise. The once star quarterback had become addicted to gambling, to the point that every team he had ever been on kicked him off and got rid of him. He had lost everything—his fortune, his luxurious home, the respect of the football community, his friends and even the girlfriends and groupies. He wound up living in his parents' basement, hidden from the world, and only left the little room to go gambling. When the last of the money ran out he borrowed large sums from some shady characters, lost all of that as well and of course couldn't pay back the debt or the ridiculous interest. He didn't want to put his parents in danger so he crept out one night, lived on the streets and hid from the loan sharks. But they eventually found him and wanted their payback.

From the grimy, wet pavement the broken man affirmatively whispered his promise. Neil said he would have the money for them in the next few days.

"If you don't, we'll find you," the bigger of the two men who had been punching him said menacingly.

"And we won't be as gentle," the other added, cackling with anticipation of the next go-around as he was sure the crumpled up man would not be able to pay.

The two goons left Neil writhing on the pavement and walked away. Neil watched them fade into the murky night and wondered where he could possibly hide, what hole he could disappear into. Would he ever be safe? Would he ever have a life again? Or was this the prelude to the end of his existence?

| | | | | | | | | | | | | | | | | | | | | | | | | | | | | | | | | | | | | | | |

CHAPTER 1  THE IDEA

| | | | | | | | | | | | | | | | | | | | | | | | | | | | | | | | | | | | | | | |

The sleek yacht moored in the Miami marina hosted her guests on the upper deck as they danced under the stars. They enjoyed themselves and followed the rhythm of the upbeat music in the warm tropical night. Her owner, William Quinn, a man in his late thirties and already a billionaire, was inside the boat's main cabin with Frank Moore. They smoked Cuban cigars, enjoyed vintage Cognac and talked sports. The older man was a billionaire as well, and some of his assets included being an owner of sports teams. He was in his sixties and considered William a nephew. Frank and the younger man's father had been best friends. They had known each other since they were teenagers when they first came from Ireland to the United States. Unfortunately William's parents had been hit by a drunk driver and killed in the collision when he was very young. Frank became his guardian and watched over little William like a loving guard dog. He had taken care of the child's inheritance trust and guided him into adulthood. The boy inherited a substantial fortune, and as a grown man was brilliant at making even more money. For the last ten years the stock market had been extremely good to him and every year he was on the list of the top ten richest men in the world.

"Great season, Uncle Frank, and congrats on winning this year's championship," William said.

"Thanks. Yeah, there's nothing like winning," Frank beamed. "Hey, how come you don't have a team, Will?"

"That's because you bought them all up."

The older man chuckled. "You should have one too. If you can't find one to buy, create one."

"Naw, I don't think so. It sounds like a lot of work," William said.

"That's why you hire pros. I bet you would like owning a team."

"I actually would," William answered truthfully, "and it would be a football team."

"That's perfect!" The older man exclaimed. "A buddy of mine wants to start up a new Chicago team, but the league needs to have two teams to balance it out. If you start up a team you would both get a green light! There are so many talented young men that try out and are sent home because the teams are limited to fifty-three players. That would be another one hundred and six very grateful athletes, not to mention how many other jobs would be created and how much the home city would reap in benefits."

Frank looked at William. He could see the younger man's eyes glowing stronger by the moment. "I'll give you up to three minutes to think about it, *boyo*," he said and chuckled. He anticipated the answer. He knew his protégé well, and as far as how much work it would be he knew William was not lazy whatsoever and would jump in with both feet.

William stared into space, or maybe it was a star through the porthole. Two minutes later he grinned and said: "Uncle Frank, where do I start?"

"What took you so long?" Frank cackled as he slapped the younger man on the back. "With the coach."

William laughed as he knew exactly who to call. He looked at the man who was his family and to whom he owed so much. He played with the cigar between his fingers and thought of his buddy, and former college roommate, Oliver Hadley. "Uncle Frank, to new adventures," William said, raising his glass. They clinked the snifters and enjoyed the excellent brandy and the melodic note of the crystal.

William watched his uncle. Frank was such a good guy, he thought, although he didn't know too much about the older man's background and how he flourished in his businesses, or the details of his early success. Frank never divulged any information, either about himself or about William's father's beginnings. The younger man always wondered about what he was sure were possibly some dubious details. Frank was a billionaire, and from what William knew, completely legitimate in his endeavors. One thing he did know about those enterprises, as it was common knowledge, was that the older man earned a percentage on anything alcoholic such as beer and whiskey that was imported to the United States from Ireland. He also never missed the opportunity to give enormous amounts to charity. To William the man was family and he knew Frank always had his back.

When the party was over and all the guests and Uncle Frank departed, William and the crew sailed out of the marina, leaving the lights of Miami and its surroundings behind them. He sat on a comfortable white leather couch on the stern. He stared blankly at the black canvas filled with winking stars above him, while his brilliant business mind calculated and assessed his new venture. After a couple of hours the peach and pink pastels of the

Florida sunrise painted the sky. When they started fading into a soft baby blue he pulled a cell phone out of his pocket and smiled. He called his best friend.

"Hello?" A sleepy voice answered.

"Hey, Oliver, it's me, Will," the man said excitedly.

"Will? What the hell time is it?"

"Sunrise, my man, a beautiful one at that."

"Where are you and what do you want at this ungodly hour? And it's my day off," he added, having just remembered.

"That's perfect! I'll be in Boston this afternoon. I'll see you at our favorite steakhouse for lunch. Let's say one o'clock."

"Will… Will?" The line was dead. What crazy idea had the man come up with this time, Oliver wondered.

William turned to his Captain. "Back to the marina, my man."

"Yes, Sir," he simply said. Neither he, nor the crew, ever minded the boss's impromptu requests. He knew the billionaire was a little eccentric, but he was a good man and a good boss. He was also very gallant with his money and made him and the other sailors happy, always giving them handsome bonuses for Christmas in addition to their good salaries, whether they were sailing with the boss or docked and taking care of the yacht. William wanted to make sure their family holidays were special. It was also the key to loyalty—listening to the ideas and needs of his employees, and respecting them.

William was back on the phone, this time with a different captain. "We're going to Boston, Scott. I need to be there by twelve thirty," he said to the pilot."

CHAPTER 2  THE COACH

The luxury private business jet, William's Cessna Citation X, touched down at Logan airport just after noon. The flight from Miami had been smooth and easy. The tycoon deplaned and got into the limousine waiting for him. The chauffeur drove out of the airport and continued into the Sumner Tunnel under Boston Harbor and into the heart of the city where he had studied as a young adult. He loved the history, the quaint old streets, the beautiful avenues, and of course the sports teams. Among them the New England Patriots. He was still a strong supporter of the organization, but he had a new fire burning in his stomach. Yes, he would be the owner of his own team. He would find a way to make it happen. Oliver Hadley, once his college roommate, would help him in his endeavor. He couldn't count the times Oliver had practically carried him back to the dorm after a terrific game and a night of boisterous and excessive indulgences. He loved the man. He was the brother he never had. He was as much family as Frank was. William had been best man at Oliver's wedding and the pain of his beautiful bride dying from cancer less than ten years later still broke his heart. He never saw Oliver serious with any other woman, maybe an occasional dinner and one night stand, but nothing more. It was as if a switch had been permanently turned off. The only consolation for the man was his stunning little girl, and he lived for her more than for himself and seemed completely satisfied with that. Roberta, who actually looked very much like her mother had was now twenty years old and graduating from Oxford University. William had already made plans to fly over to England to attend the ceremony at the end of spring.

William arrived at the restaurant first and sat down at a table with a view of Newbury Street. He placed an order with the waiter and looked at his watch. He smiled. Oliver was more prompt than the English when it came to being on time. He was never, ever late. He knew his buddy would be walking up to him in the next sixty seconds. True to his style Oliver slapped William on the shoulder and the two men gave each other great bear hugs. They were always happy to see each other. Just like William the native Bostonian was in his late thirties, with a few gray hairs in his temples giving him an elegant appearance to match his rugged good looks. And he was fit. He loved sports and working out, and never missed an opportunity to play or exercise, not professionally but for pleasure and to keep in shape.

A few minutes later their order arrived—the biggest steak in the city decorated by their favorite sides and paired with a stellar wine.

"Perfect, as always," Oliver chuckled, smelling the aroma wafting up to him from his plate.

"Don't ever become a spy, man, you're much too predictable."

"Yeah, I guess."

"Speaking of jobs, you're still with the Pats, right?"

"I am."

Oliver was an assistant coach for the New England team. He was one of the youngest coaches in the football league and very much in demand, but Oliver was loyal. He was born and raised in Boston and was enjoying his dream job. Why would he ever go elsewhere, even if the money was better? Money wasn't that important. What he made was more than sufficient. Oliver would love to be head coach somewhere, in due time perhaps, but there wasn't anything out there that really seemed attractive. He was happy where he was.

"When is your contract up with them?" William asked.

"I have to renew in the next few weeks."

William smiled. He was getting that gut feeling he always got when something was falling into place. "I see."

"You see what?" Oliver asked. He knew William too well. He was up to something.

"Which means you're pretty much free."

"You mean as in a job?"

"Uh, huh."

"Alright, Will, spit it out and why did you want to see me? What is that wicked mind of yours concocting?"

"Can't I just have a nice lunch with a good buddy?"

"Of course, now spill."

"I need you, my friend."

"Well, that goes without say. I'm always here for you, man. Is everything okay? Or is this another of your crazy ideas?"

"Yes, everything is good, thanks, and yes this is another of my totally awesome ideas."

"Uh, oh."

"You're going to love it!"

"Double oh, oh. Sounds like you want to involve *me* in those wicked ideas."

"I do and *you* are going to be the most important

piece," William said matter-of-factly.

"Would you spit it out already and tell me what the hell you're trying to cook up?"

"Chicago is trying to build a new football team."

"Yeah, I heard about that, but they're not going anywhere without a second team to balance the league out."

"Exactly. That's where we come in."

Oliver stared at William for a long moment and then started laughing, hard. "Are you telling me that *you're* the other team?" he asked between breaths.

William grinned, a big Cheshire cat grin.

"And what do you mean by *we*?"

"You and me. I'm the cash, you're the football brains and the head coach."

Oliver looked at him. What the man was saying was really nice but it was just a dream, actually it was more of a nightmare. "You can't be serious, Will. Do you have any idea what's involved?"

"Somewhat."

Oliver groaned. "Look, this is an amazing idea…"

"Yeah, right?" William said excitedly.

"Will, pay attention!"

"I am. Just tell me what you need."

"Oh, my God, you're serious."

"Dead."

"Dead what?"

"Dead serious. Come on, Oliver, humor me. What would you need? We already have a coach, you, and your salary would quadruple and you would be ten percent owner of the team, and its profits of course."

"Yeah, that's nice," Oliver said, dismissing William's input. He had to get through to him, although remembering their university days he knew that wouldn't be easy. When the man put his mind to something he became as stubborn as a bull in a corrida. "Alright, off the top of my head you need a coach. We'll say that's me. Then you need staff and of course, the players."

"That's the easy part."

"What? How do you figure? All the players are either under contract or already trying out for the next season. There aren't any available. If there were, we would have to find them, put the word out."

"No problem. You know all those fine players that just didn't quite make the cut? Imagine how happy they would be to be part of a team."

Oliver just shook his head. "Will…" He started.

"As for staff. Do you know of anyone who *wouldn't* want to be part of a football team? From the water boy to the equipment handlers and doctors. And money moves mountains. They would get paid better than any other team. As far as the players, all you need is a really good guy, who you probably already know, to go out and find the players we need. The two of you would recruit together. I know how brilliant you are. You would assemble one the best teams ever!"

Oliver watched William—a bulldog with a toy he wasn't about to let go of. Oliver's mind was reeling. "This a huge endeavor, Will," Oliver said, overwhelmed by the scope of all of it.

"Don't think of it as a mountain, rather the mountain already exists and all we have to do is 'decorate' it with a few trees and bushes.

Oliver was only half listening to William as his mind was already analyzing and yes, he had someone in mind to find the players—George Bunson. The man probably knew everything there was to know about a body playing with a football. He could immediately pick up on a player's assets and make him better. Oliver in turn was the maestro. He would come in afterward and would fine tune them like a classical orchestra. The two of them had worked together before and always brought good results. As much fun as all this would be Oliver feared it was just impossible, and completely overwhelming.

"Sorry, Will, this is just too big, too much. It's just such an enormous endeavor...

"You have someone in mind, don't you, Oliver?" William said, cutting him off. He knew how to whet his buddy's appetite.

"Yeah, George Bunson."

"Ah, yes, Uncle Frank did mention him. I have faith in you, Oliver, you can do this. We can do this!"

"How is Uncle Frank?" Oliver asked, trying to ease out and change the conversation.

"He's good. He's actually the one who put the idea in my head."

"Oh, Uncle Frank, you didn't!"

"You will have anything you want," William continued. "Hire whatever staff you need, who in turn will help you in their own field. You get George and the three of us will sit down and hammer all the details out. I will get the financing and everything like that."

Everything like that. Oh, brother, Will had no idea what all this entailed. "And when do you want answers to all of this?" Oliver asked.

"Tomorrow morning," William said, getting up. He had of course already paid the waiter when he came in. "I'm going to the hotel to get some sleep. I've been up all night." William patted Oliver on his shoulder as he made his way to the exit.

"I'm sure you have. I'll call you," Oliver said. He watched his friend crossing the street on his way to the luxurious hotel. He sat there immobile, staring blankly through the window for a solid twenty minutes, and then dialed a number.

"Roberta? Hi, Sweetheart."

"Hi, Daddy, what's up?" Oliver could hear her perfectly, even though she was a little over three thousand miles away.

"No how are you, how's the weather, etcetera? Why would you think anything is up?"

"I can always tell."

Oliver giggled. He loved his relationship with his daughter. He took a deep breath and told Roberta about William. When he finished he added: "I would like to go for it. Would that be okay with you?"

"Of course it would. I think it's a wonderful idea. Definitely go for it!"

"Yeah?"

"Absolutely. You and Uncle Will together can't go wrong. You will pull it off brilliantly!"

The next phone call Oliver made was to his longtime friend and sidekick George Bunson. The man was a specialist and a legend. He had the amazing talent of seeing a player's potential even before the player himself knew what he was capable of. He could just look at the way they walked, ran or positioned themselves on the field. He watched the way they held their hands around a football, whether they were touching it or catching it. Bunson could look at a player's body and decipher where he would fit best. He was hardly ever wrong and could hone those bodies to fit a position perfectly and bring out the best they could ever be. He had worked with national franchises helping them recruit the best possible talent teams. The past year had been his last before he retired.

"George?"

"Hey, Oliver, how are you?" The older man replied, genuinely happy to hear from his good friend.

"I'm good. How about you? How's retirement?"

"It's nice," he answered flatly.

"Nice?" Oliver repeated. "Retirement should be a little more exciting than that, shouldn't it?"

"Well, truth be told, I'm bored out of my mind. And Christ, I miss the smell of it all."

Oliver chuckled. "George, can you meet me? I'm about to throw you the craziest idea you've ever heard and I'd like your opinion."

"I presume it has something to do with football?" George asked hopefully.

"Oh, yes, it most certainly does."

CHAPTER 3  THE TEAM DREAM

The next morning Oliver called his best man. William already knew the answer when the phone rang, but he smiled as the man on the other end of the line confirmed that both he and George were in.

"Why don't you two come by at eight tomorrow morning? We'll have breakfast in my room. I have a few calls to make," William said.

"Yeah, we do too. See you then, Will."

They hung up. Both William and Oliver, one from a hotel suite, the other from a home office, pumped their arms in the air and jumped a foot off the floor. They had both scored their own individual touchdowns.

William went to the desk and looked at the notepad and the list of calls he had to make. He sat down, got comfortable and started dialing the first number.

Oliver did the exact same thing from his house. George, on the other hand, who had slept there after an exhaustive all night session with Oliver, was already on the phone. His working manner totally different from that of the other two men. He was slumped in an armchair already talking into the receiver, a pad in his lap and papers strewn around his feet.

The three men focused their efforts throughout the day.

The next morning they convened in William's room. True to form they were there promptly at eight and Oliver introduced George to his old friend. A sumptuous breakfast buffet was set up for them which arrived after just a few minutes. They indulged their palates and stomachs and immediately started talking.

"Hey, I read about you in Forbes. You're one of the richest men…" George stopped himself.

"I'm a rich, wacky guy with a team dream. Yeah, I can see that. You think this is just a toy for me, right?" William looked at the older man. "Let me assure you, both of you. I'm dead serious about this team and I will be present one hundred percent. I won't let you, or anyone connected with this endeavor, down. I want you to know that you can call me 24/7 and I will do my best. I love football and I already love this team we are building. I *want* it to succeed. I'm a big dreamer and I love to win. You won't find anyone more competitive than me. Who knows how far we can take this? My mindset is always 'all the way'."

Both Oliver and George were listening intently. William continued: "George, I've known Oliver for a long time and he is a brother to me. I have complete confidence in him, which also means if he chose you I have no doubts about you either. I've of course learned about you too, George, and I know we'll get along great."

George wasn't surprised. Of course this powerful man would know everything about him, maybe even the polka dot underwear his wife always gave him at Christmas. "Then you know that I'm the most loyal man you'll ever meet," George emphasized.

"I do know that, and I'm really happy that we're all on the same team—literally. I want you to think of me as a partner, never a boss."

"I appreciate that," George said and held out his hand.

William shook it and held it. He put out his other hand and Oliver shook that one. They were all holding hands. It was a bond they would work hard to maintain strong and special.

"Alright, here's what I worked on yesterday," William said to the men as they all sat around a table. He told them about the financing, although the man was so wealthy he didn't need any bank's money, but he had spoken to his uncle who had made some sound suggestions.

Oliver and George were duly impressed. They in turn relayed what they had done.

"I've got a bunch of players lined up for tryouts," George said. "I didn't tell them how much they would be making or what city the team would be located in. They're probably thinking we'll be in Florida… uh, just where exactly…"

William was anticipating the question. The answer would probably land on them and explode like an enormous water balloon. "Albuquerque."

They stared at him. Oliver finally found his voice. "New Mexico?"

William nodded.

"As in between Texas and Arizona?" Oliver followed up, still dumbfounded, wanting to make sure he had heard right.

"Actually," George said, "that's not bad."

William raised his eyebrow and smiled. The man was sharp.

"It's not?" Oliver asked.

"Well, the way I figure, New Mexico doesn't have a team…"

"It doesn't have any people either. I mean, not enough for the marketing support that is needed."

"You're not wrong, Oliver," William said, "however, the NFL has always wanted to tap into the Mexican market somehow, which is huge. They would love if Mexico City would have a team in the league, however, there are too many problems, and least of all it's a different country with difficult laws. Texas has teams even though they thought San Antonio might have a shot, but New Mexico is just next door and it has *Mexico* in the name."

"But what about a stadium? You have to have a venue that can hold at least 50,000 spectators," Oliver said.

"Yes, that's true, but building a new stadium is really expensive and takes much too long." William looked at them and grinned. "The University of New Mexico has a stadium that can seat almost 40,000. I spoke to the mayor."

"Of course you did," Oliver said.

"And guess what?" William asked the two men sitting across from him.

"What?" They asked at the same time.

"The city will foot the bill, fifty million dollars, to expand the stadium at UNM."

"They already agreed on that? How is that even possible?" Oliver asked, although he knew better. William could move mountains.

"I have really good contacts and explained the financial boost to New Mexico and Albuquerque," William answered. He thought of his uncle and smiled. "I also gave them a guarantee that if our team doesn't work out I will reimburse them half, twenty-five million."

Oliver whistled.

George let out a groan and said: "I don't like losing anything, whether it's a game or money. We *are* going to make this a success!"

"As the cliché says, money can't buy you love, but it sure can get things accomplished fast," William said.

"That's for sure!" George said.

The three men hollered, cheered and high-fived each other. Their enthusiasm and energy was on a record high level.

CHAPTER 4 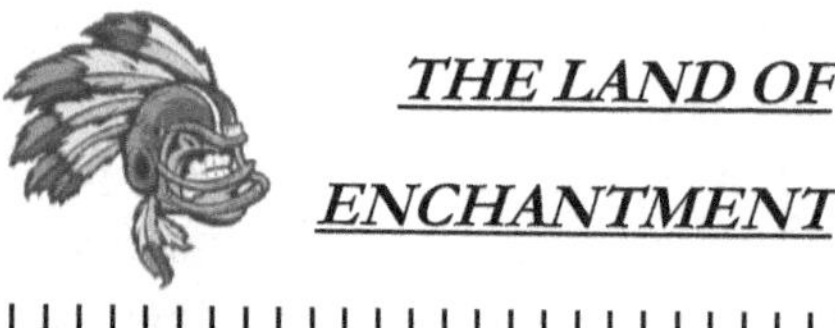 THE LAND OF ENCHANTMENT

Oliver, George, William and two of his lawyers were hard at work finishing last minute details as they descended through the clouds above the high desert of New Mexico. They were flying into Albuquerque to meet with city and university officials. William would be the one ironing out the legal and financial specifics and meeting with the mayor and his staff. Oliver and George would be there as well, but their main focus after the initial meeting would be interviewing potential players invited for tryouts. William bought every prospective member a ticket to fly in for the event. Their meals and hotel rooms were paid for as well. The players had nothing to lose. If they made the team they would be living their dream. If they didn't, they would have had a nice little vacation, all expenses paid. Oliver and George would meet the players on the field in a couple of days and evaluate the possibilities and their performances.

Before landing they marveled at the landscape. Mountains and desert vistas seemed to welcome them to the land they called Enchanted. The Citation X landed smoothly at Albuquerque's Sunport. They came out of the jet and walked toward the limousine waiting for them.

"Holy shit! How hot is it?" George gasped as the dry

air hit him like a Swedish sauna. It just happened to be uncommonly hot for that time of year.

"Hot. And the air is really thin," Oliver grumbled.

"That's because we're over five thousand feet, a little higher than Denver," William commented.

"We're going to need more oxygen," George groaned.

"Uh, huh," Oliver agreed.

"Come on guys," William coaxed them on, "let's discover New Mexico!"

"Where does the man get his energy?" The older man whispered.

"New adventure," Oliver answered.

The three men entered the cool car waiting for them on the tarmac and the chauffeur took them to the Mayor's office at City Hall. UNM's Dean and some of his staff were also present. Everyone who needed to be there did not miss the meeting. It would be one of the city's most important ones. Albuquerque and New Mexico needed a really big boost to their economy and it came to them in the form of William Quinn and the future local team. They all exchanged greetings and pleasantries and very quickly got down to business. Their meeting was successful and once finished they continued on to the University of New Mexico and out to the stadium. Oliver and George looked at each other. They of course weren't expecting Michigan Stadium or Beaver Stadium and the UNM field was like a smaller sibling, albeit the cutest one. It was quaint and cozy. The extension to add the required seating wouldn't hinder any of its charm.

They continued the planning in the director's office. At some point Oliver said his goodbyes and left to meet up with George and finish some preparations for the following day's tryouts.

"Dean," William said, "I'm looking for someone local, who knows the ins and outs of the city, the campus, and who is quick and sharp.

"Oh, that's easy, Dezba Yazzie. "She's one of our best students. She received a hard-earned scholarship which put her through the years she needed to get her to graduation, which she will do this year. She's finished with her classes and is just helping out the university. She would be a big help to you. She's a Navajo, fluent in both languages as well as Spanish, and a pillar of the community. Anything you need or want to know she probably already knows or can find out."

"Sounds like just what I need. Where can I meet her?"

"I'll have her sent up," the Dean said as he reached for his phone.

A few minutes later they heard a knock on the door.

"Come in," the Dean cried.

Dezba walked in. "You wanted to see me, Dean?"

The men stood as the woman walked in. She nodded to them. William smiled. She wasn't quite what he had pictured. He was, however, very pleasantly surprised. He had imagined a twenty year old student, instead he figured this woman was around thirty. She went to the Dean's desk and as she did William couldn't help noticing a natural air of nobility when she walked over. Maybe it was just an elegant physical glide, or perhaps a Navajo pride. And her hair! It was so black and shiny it shone streaks of blue. Her eyes were very dark and slightly almond shaped, and when she smiled William was sure light would emanate through her smooth lips. She wasn't a classic beauty, but the ensemble of her lovely assets made her extremely attractive, so much so that people would want to immediately get to know her. William was instantly one of those people.

"Yes, Dezba," the Dean said, "I would like you to meet Mr. William Quinn."

William took a couple of steps toward her and shook her hand. "Very pleased to meet you."

"Pleased to meet you too." *Why was he here,* she wondered. *Who was he?* She quickly assessed the man. He was tall, thin, elegant and wore nice clothes. She found him good looking with green eyes that reminded her of liquid jade and an easy comforting manner.

"Dezba, this gentleman just arrived in town and doesn't know much about Albuquerque or New Mexico. He has become, however, a very important man in our community and needs some information. I thought you might be able to help him out."

What am I now, a tour guide?

As if reading her mind William quickly jumped in: "I hope you don't mind. I would be very grateful if you could help me out and you will be compensated, of course."

Oh, why not, she thought, *it would be a change of atmosphere and I can use the money. He looks like a decent enough guy.* "I guess I could do that," she answered.

"Thank you, Dezba, that's very gracious of you," the Dean said.

"My pleasure."

"Yes, thank you very much. I really appreciate it," William added.

"One thing, Dezba," the Dean said very seriously.

"Yes?"

"Any conversation with Mr. Quinn and any information you will talk about is to be strictly confidential. Can I count on you?"

"Absolutely. There won't be any problem."

"Excellent, thank you, Dezba."

"Yes, thank you very much," William repeated. "Is there anywhere we could get something to eat? Maybe a cafeteria or a little restaurant nearby?"

"Yeah, sure, there's one right across from the university. Come on, I'll take you over."

"Great! I'm famished. Would you like to join us?" He asked the head of the university who declined. "Thank you for everything, Dean. We'll talk very soon."

Dezba headed out and William followed her. Depending if he turned out to be an ass, or not, she would introduce him to what she thought would be the appropriate heat level of the famous local chile peppers.

The native woman and William walked across the street to a local hangout, famous for its New Mexican food and frequented by locals, students and inquisitive tourists.

When they walked in William knew without a question he was in the Southwest. Pictures and paintings of John Wayne, cowboys and desert landscapes greeted him from every wall. He liked the atmosphere of the people around him. They were of all ages and walks of life, and without exception enjoying good traditional food.

"What do you suggest? There are so many choices!" William asked as he looked at the menu.

"Do you have preference, or something you don't particularly like?"

"No, no problem with anything." William was a connoisseur when it came to food, and he loved everything from caviar to corn dogs. He wasn't picky and loved discovering new cuisines.

"Shall I pick something out?"

"Oh, yes, please do."

"Okay." Dezba put in the order. The waiter brought it over when it was ready. The portions were enormous.

"Oh, my, this is huge!" William exclaimed.

"You get your money's worth."

"That's an understatement, and it looks delicious! Tell me, what's in it?" William asked as he was sure the burrito surrounded by frijoles and rice was filled with something mouth-watering.

"The burrito is filled with carne adovada which is slow cooked pork that has been marinated in red chile sauce," Dezba explained. As she did she noticed those green eyes. They were filled with child-like excitement, as if he had been presented with a new toy. "Try it."

William did. He loved every bite he took and told Dezba how much he enjoyed it. She was glad he liked what she had ordered for him. They enjoyed their meal and made small talk, Dezba mainly explaining the area and anything William wanted to know about the Land of Enchantment.

In addition to being brilliant in how to make money William had another asset—he had a sixth sense about a person's character. As far as Dezba his mind had been made up after about two minutes with her, as if the man could look right into her soul. He liked what he saw and he wanted to know everything about her.

"The Dean told me you will be graduating this year," William said.

"That's right."

"What's your major?"

"Business and economics."

"Great field. Any particular reason why you chose that?"

Dezba looked into those green pools. The man actually was interested, and not just trying to make small talk. Besides, it wasn't a secret. "I find it fascinating and a good way to help my people on the Reservation. I believe the success of everything is knowledge and especially education. It opens people's minds and their focus. I want to try to install that in them and help them to help themselves, maybe try their hand at their own business, whether it's a fruit stand or building homes."

"That's smart and very noble. I predict you will go far."

"Kind of you to say."

"I mean it. It only takes one spark to start fireworks and I predict you will make beautiful designs in the sky, for you and your people."

Dezba was liking William more by the minute. He was polite and attentive, and he wasn't trying to show off like most men she knew who always tried to prove they were somebody, especially if they were wealthy. "Thank you, Mr. Quinn."

"Oh, no, that won't do at all, the name's William."

"Okay, William, I can do that."

"Good. And what else do you do beside go to school and study?" He was curious to know if she was married or had a boyfriend. He didn't see a ring.

"I work."

"May I ask what you do?"

"I manage a new apartment complex. It's just been built and the owners want to start selling the apartments."

"Is it here in town?"

"It's close, near the airport, which as you know is only about ten minutes from downtown and the university. It's located in a fairly deserted area with bare land all around it. It has magnificent views of the city and the mesa." Was he interested in buying one of the apartments? She hoped so as she would get a nice commission. "Are you looking to buy something?" She asked.

"I might be. How many apartments are there in the building?"

"Sixty-six. The owners thought that would make it very Southwestern and New Mexican, you know Route 66 and all that."

"Got it. Can we go there? I'd like to see it, and maybe an apartment as well." William had an idea brewing and wanted to see if it could come to fruition, but more importantly he wanted to spend additional time with Dezba and maybe help her at the same time.

"Sure," she answered, thrilled at the possibility, "I have a master key."

"Excellent, and thank you for the delicious meal. My tummy is very happy," he said boyishly, patting his stomach.

"I'm glad," she chuckled.

William cherished Dezba's mind, ambitious energy and her ease. She was a serious person, but he knew there was also a fun side just dying to emerge. He hoped she would share that with him. He hoped she would share many things with him.

They left the restaurant and went to the limousine. William made sure the chauffeur had lunch when they had and after a few directions from Dezba they were off to the apartment complex.

When they arrived they emerged from the car. William looked around at the vast expanse of barren land. There were miles of untouched desert wilderness just outside the city. The only exception was the building which of course boasted magnificent vistas from every apartment.

"This is it," Dezba announced.

"And you are the keeper?"

"I am. I oversee the running of the project."

"Which includes selling units."

"Right. And making sure problems get resolved, such as calling maintenance people if needed or whatever may arise."

"And I'm sure you're very good at it," William added.

"I try, and it's a pretty good job. Come on, I'll take you around."

"Sounds great. I like this place." It was even better than William had hoped for.

Dezba was happy to hear that. She took him around the complex and showed him a couple of the apartments. He seemed to be quite interested, especially in the top floor. William stared out the window. He could see the mesa, the city and the airport. He stopped looking around. He had formed a plan in his mind. He asked Dezba a few questions about the complex and the surrounding land.

Dezba saw a glow in William's eyes she hadn't noticed before. She would, in just a short period of time, come to recognize the meaning of that particular shine. When the man went after something he wanted and was on the verge of success the glow was at its brightest, and at this very moment that is exactly what his eyes conveyed.

William made a call to the lawyers who had flown in with him and told them exactly what he wanted. He was standing in the main room of the penthouse floor. There were more windows than walls and the views were breathtaking. He hung up with them and turned to Dezba. He took in her pretty face and desperately wanted to touch her exquisite lips, but he didn't want to seem hasty. Although William was not usually a patient man he knew that when he wanted something as special as this woman he could be extremely patient.

"Where do you live, Dezba?" He asked.

"I rent a studio close to the campus. It's small but adequate and when my brother Ahiga comes to town he stays with me. It gets a little cramped, but we manage. We're very close. It's been just the two of us for many years."

"Where does he come from?"

"From the Reservation, it's about an hour away."

"Do you have a car?"

"I do. Actually Ahiga and I share it, and it's an antique."

"Really? William loved antique cars and boasted several of his own. What kind?"

"A twenty year old pickup with over 250,000 miles on it."

William whistled. "That's not exactly what I was expecting. Although I'm impressed it's still running."

"My father bought it, used of course, when I was ten. I learned how to drive in it and it's been my wheels ever since. I can't bring myself to get rid of it even though I know it might die on me at any moment. It's on its last legs, poor thing. It's like an old horse."

"You're sentimental," William said, liking this woman more by the minute.

"I am, but it's also my mode of transportation. Ahiga and I use it to go back and forth to the Rez."

William wanted to learn everything about Dezba and her life. They spent most of the day together. By late afternoon they were eating dinner, their endeavors making them hungry. Over a delicious meal William made the Navajo woman feel completely at ease and she told William her life story, from childhood to this moment. The man was impressed with her fighting spirit, how she never gave up and how she was trying to better not only her own life but her brother's. William liked every single thing about her, from her lovely features to her determination. He was falling for her and wanted to spend as much time together as he possibly could. He of course wanted her in more than one way, but as much as he loved quickly acquiring material things he wanted whatever time was needed to let their feelings take their course.

At the end of the evening the limousine took them to her studio. They both got out of the car and looked at each other. They knew they wanted to kiss one another but William did not push. He didn't want to seem forward. He took one of her hands and kissed it. "It's been a wonderful day and you've been an incredible help. Thank you, Dezba."

"It was my pleasure, William. If there's anything else I can help with please let me know."

"I know I have many more questions and much to discover in this beautiful part of the world. Would you be available tomorrow?"

"Yes, that wouldn't be a problem. I'll call the Dean. He's a good guy."

"Yes, he is. That's great. Pick you up at eight? Is that okay?"

"Perfect."

"Alright, I'll see you in the morning," William said as he started turning around.

"William?"

The man's heart skipped a beat. "Yes?" He turned back to face her and looked deep into the cocoa-colored eyes. They reminded him of a gentle doe.

"I had a wonderful day, thank you." Dezba went up to him and kissed him lightly on the lips. She had been wanting to do that most of the day. She had never felt this close this fast to any man before. When they parted they just looked at each and then kissed again, this time with much more passion.

"I'll see you tomorrow. Shall we do breakfast?" William asked as he entered the limousine. It was the earliest he could think of. How was he going to get through the night? She nodded and he watched her enter the studio apartment and signaled to the chauffeur to go to the hotel where he was staying.

The next morning the limousine arrived at the agreed time and they headed to a restaurant for breakfast. When Dezba sat next to William he kissed her cheek. She tenderly took his face in her hands and kissed his lips. When they parted she asked: "Did you sleep well?"

"Actually, no, I couldn't sleep. I was thinking about you," William answered truthfully.

"I had the same problem."

They came together again and kissed passionately.

William's cell phone rang. He hated parting with Dezba's amazing lips but looked at the little screen. It was the call he was waiting for. "I'm sorry, I have to take this."

"Go right ahead. I'll be right here," she said, smiling.

"Yes?" He said into the phone. It was the lawyers. He listened for a few moments and smiled—the deal had gone through. "Thank you both, great job!" He hung up and turned to face Dezba! "It's done!" He said excitedly.

"What's done?" She looked at William's eyes and saw the same glow he'd had yesterday. Something good must have happened.

"My ideas and plans were confirmed, and you had a major part in it."

"I did?"

"Yes, my lawyers just told me that your apartment complex owner has agreed to my terms."

"How do you mean?" *Had he bought the apartment they looked at?*

"I bought it."

"The apartment?"

"No, the building," he said and kissed her.

Dezba imagined she would get a commission on the sale of the apartment, but would she also get something for the entire building? If she did it would change her life considerably.

William gave her the answer: "You will of course get a commission for the sale of the entire building and also the surrounding land."

"The surrounding land?" She repeated.

"Yes, it was a good investment and much cheaper than I anticipated. All in all a very good deal."

Dezba's lungs were ready to burst. She had just made more money in an instant than she would have made in at least ten years.

"And it's close to the airport hangars we leased," William continued.

"What hangars?"

"Right off the airport. They're both very large. One is for the Citation X, and the other is where we will be training. We're converting it into the team's training facility with a locker room, meeting room, workout room and of course large enough for practices."

The man moved so damn fast! "You are amazing, William Quinn." Dezba's head was spinning. But she loved the way he went after his dream and got results. She liked everything about him, and oh, was the man a good kisser!

"Thank you, Dezba. Now, I have a couple of questions for you."

"Go right ahead."

"Well, you're out of a job."

"I am?"

"Yes, from the apartment complex."

"How come?" She asked, wondering where he was going with this.

"Well, there are no apartments to sell anymore."

"That's true, but what about the maintenance?"

"We can get somebody else for that."

"I see." She didn't.

"But I would like to offer you a different job."

"Oh? Doing what exactly?" Dezba wondered.

"To be my right hand. I need someone local, who knows everything about New Mexico and Albuquerque. Someone who can get things done, who is wise and full of energy and determination."

Dezba wasn't saying anything, she was just listening. She looked at him, thrilled with the offer.

"And I'm selfish," he added. "I want you close to me."

Oh, she wanted that too. "Are kisses included, boss?"

"An infinite and constant amount of them."

"Then I accept, and with pleasure."

"Oh, did I mention the job pays six figures?"

Dezba was in a dream. Her life had just completely changed and… what had he just said? Six figures? She had worked so hard her entire life to get ahead, fought to help her brother and get a good education. She needed the money badly and had struggled for years to make her dreams and goals come to fruition, but at this moment she could only think of William's lips.

CHAPTER 5   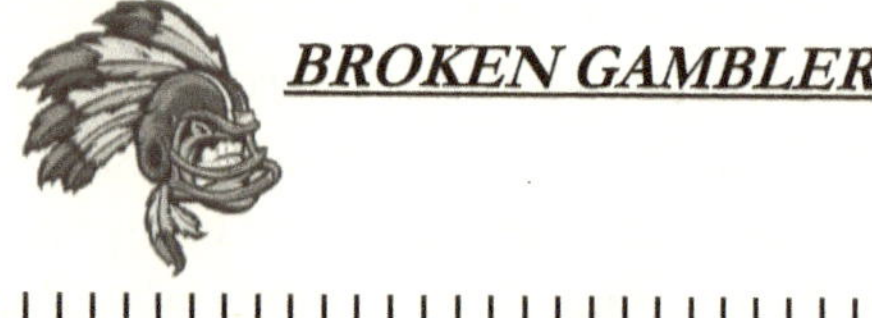   BROKEN GAMBLER

"You can't be serious!" George groaned.

"Completely," Oliver answered. "Look, I never met a guy who loved the game of football more than Neil Howard, nor a better quarterback. He was a dual-threat, great at passing and rushing, and a hell of a runner when needed. He was a natural leader with a God-given talent. His arm was one of the best in the league and he could probably have followed in the footsteps of the greats and racked up quite a few records."

"All very true. Unfortunately he found a game he loved even more: gambling. He's been kicked off every team he ever played for, and no one wants to take a chance on him. He's unreliable, Oliver, don't even think about him."

"I know, but he's brilliant. He reminds me of Drew Brees."

"I agree, however, Brees is brilliant *and* reliable," George intonated, "in every way."

"I want a meeting with Howard."

The older man shook his head and tried to dissuade him. "Oh, Oliver, he's a loose cannon. You just can't trust him," he moaned.

"And his arm is like a cannon too."

"Geez, Oliver, I don't even know if he's alive. I heard some bad stuff happened to him. It's like he's disappeared."

"Now, George…"

"Okay, okay, I'll get him."

"Great. Thanks."

"Uh, huh."

Finding Neil Howard hadn't been an easy task as he had been in hiding. With a little help from William and his connections one of the best investigators in the business was hired to find him. The man and his associates tracked him down pretty quickly. They found Neil hiding in a crack house barricaded behind a rancid futon. The dark and putrid rooms housed passed out or blank-staring addicts strewn on filthy mattresses among discarded needles, vomit and other waste. As tough as the investigators were they could feel their stomach churning. They pulled Neil from behind his makeshift rampart and lifted him up. They realized that he thankfully wasn't into drugs and figured the man thought the goons wouldn't look for him in a place of lost souls, although Neil wasn't far from joining the despair. They convinced him they were there to help and not to harm him. They cleaned him up and brought him to New Mexico and Oliver.

When Neal entered the hotel room Oliver was staying in the coach almost didn't recognize the once brilliant quarterback. The younger man was thinner than he remembered. He looked haggard, run down, with sagging bags under his eyes and Oliver detected a trace of fear in them as well.

"Hi, I'm Oliver Hadley," he said, putting out his hand.

Neal immediately shook it. "I know who you are, Coach, nice to meet you."

"Looks like you ran into a door, or maybe someone ran into you," Oliver said, looking at the ugly bruises and welts on the man's face even through the unkempt, scrawny beard. Howard was also known for his good looks and always made the list of handsome quarterbacks like Tom Brady, Cam Newton and Aaron Rodgers, but the man in front of him wasn't anywhere close to his once attractive features.

"Quarterbacks aren't supposed to get banged up like that. That's what the rest of the team protects first and foremost."

"Yeah, you're right, Coach, but I didn't have a team with me."

"A man without a team." Oliver stared at him for a few moments, just enough to make Neal uneasy. "You love the game, don't you Neal?"

"Yes, Sir, more than anything."

"No, I don't think so. Maybe some time ago, but lately you've forgotten about football and found something you love even more, or perhaps I should say are addicted to."

There was no use in lying, Neal was sure Coach Hadley knew everything about him. "Yes, sir," he whispered, lowering his eyes.

"Do you have any money left?"

"No, Sir."

"You've been staying at your parents' house?"

Neal nodded, embarrassed that a world famous and amazing quarterback had reduced himself to a renegade teenager still living at home. "I was for a while until..." Neil stopped, too ashamed.

"Until the sharks found you and wanted their money back," Oliver finished for him. He knew about the goons who had been chasing him. "I know you love the game, Neal, but answer me this: Do you still love throwing? Do you still love winning?" Oliver immediately noticed the sudden shine in the younger man's eyes.

"More than anything, Coach."

"Would you still want to play?" Oliver asked slowly.

Almost in tears, as he knew he had blown every chance ever given to him and that he would never play professionally again, all Neil could do was look at the floor and slowly nod.

"Would you want to play for me?"

Neil looked up. Was he serious? He knew the coach was an assistant on the New England Patriots' team. "For the Pats?"

Oliver shook his head. "No, for the New Mexico Natives."

"Who?" Neil asked, the happy balloon growing in his lungs deflating wildly.

"It's a new NFL team, based here. I was offered the head coach position and I'm assembling players. I'd like it if you joined us."

Neil didn't know what to do. He was on the run, something the coach probably knew since he was brought here. He didn't know who the Natives were, but playing was playing. It seemed fresh and new, and he liked Hadley. How would he put himself in the spotlight with the goons after him? He would never be able to assemble enough money to pay off what he owed, which of course was greatly overdue and accumulating ridiculous interest.

As if reading his mind Oliver continued: "If you make it through the season a million bucks will be put in your bank account. It's not what you're used to and a little unorthodox, but it's a fresh start. Money in the bank, no headaches, you get to play, and you earn your freedom. Not just for you but for your parents, who are certainly scared shitless for their son's life and probably for their own as well. Your debt would be taken care of and the loan sharks off your ass. You would be free to live your life."

Neil's stomach knotted in pain at the thought of the fear and misery he put his parents through. He would do it. He would be the best player he could be and follow the coach's direction, but most of all he would do it for his parents. They had always been loving and supporting, and as they headed toward the autumn of their lives they deserved the very best from their son. "I'll do it, coach, with great pleasure and all my thanks."

"I'm going to be counting on you, Neil. If everything goes well we'll talk at the end of the season about future contracts."

"That sounds fine, Coach."

"And I do have some conditions."

"Of course, Coach." Here it comes, Neal thought.

"Absolutely no gambling. I don't even want to see a shell game."

"Understood, Coach."

"I want you to be very sure about that because if you stray even once, especially in a state that has casinos all over the damn place, those goons that have been after you will seem like Mother Teresas. Understand?"

Neil looked at his new coach. The man was dead serious. "Yes, Coach."

"Good. One more thing: I know this is going to be really hard. An addiction is an addiction and when times are tough, and there will be, I want you to come to me. I don't want you to think that there isn't anything I can do to help. You don't know what I can do or how I can help you. That's part of this deal."

"Yes, Coach, thank you."

"Also, the owner, William Quinn, has invested a great

deal of money in getting this team going. He has an apartment complex for the players and staff. You get your own place rent free so you don't have to worry about that either.

Neal was speechless. Why, when he had been such an ass, was he now getting a second chance? "Thank you, Coach, and Mr. Quinn of course."

"Good, that's settled. Is there anything you want to ask me, or anything you need at this time?"

Neil really did want to know why Hadley was giving him such a chance, such a gift, but he didn't ask. "No, Coach. Just thank you for giving me back my life."

As if Oliver were reading his mind he added: "I believe in second chances. Don't fuck this one up, Neil."

"I won't, Coach, I won't let you down."

"I have faith in you. I want you to revert to the brilliant player you once were and to lead this new team. I need a really strong leader, Neil. Victories are always welcome and our main goal, but good playing and a great heart are what's most important, and that's what it's going to take. Are we in agreement?"

"Absolutely, Coach."

"Welcome to the family," Oliver said and held out his hand.

Neil immediately shook it. He looked into the eyes of the man giving him a second chance at life and said: "May I hug you, Coach?"

"Absolutely," Oliver grinned, and gave his new quarterback a huge bear hug. His gut told him this was the beginning of a prolific relationship.

||||||||||||||||||||||||||||||||||||||||||||||||

CHAPTER 6      TRYOUTS

||||||||||||||||||||||||||||||||||||||||||||||||

The coaches, staff and hopeful players were all present for the tryouts. The atmosphere was thick with anticipation and the possibility of fulfilling dreams of a professional career in football, particularly for the players who had tried out for other teams and didn't make it during the NFL Scouting Combine.

Oliver and George looked at the young men on the field waiting for instructions.

"There's quite a bit of talent here today," Oliver said.

"Yeah, there is. Now we just need to weed out the best ones and make a team of them."

"There's nothing like making someone's dream come true, especially if they are deserving. Some of these guys will be the first players of the New Mexico Natives. We need them to be special. An added bonus will be how much team spirit they have, and just as important would be their character."

"Yeah, I agree with that. I never could stand those stuck up sons-of-bitches, no matter what talent they had," George agreed.

"Well, let's see what we've got, my friend. Today we start history and our first year."

They looked at each other and shook hands. They were as excited as the players. This was the beginning of a new professional team.

George had all the players warm up, stretch and do bursts before putting them through the different drills. The players weren't wearing any helmets or uniforms, rather they were in t-shirts and shorts. This wasn't a practice with tackling or hitting.

George separated the receivers, the defensive backs and the big guys and sent them to their pertinent coaches.

Oliver and George watched their assistants put the players through their appropriate drills. They watched them closely and took notes as the players did forty-yard dashes, broad jumps as well as vertical jumps. They also followed meticulously when they did lateral runs, stopping and starting with bursts of speed for the twenty and sixty yard shuttles. The players also showed their prowess in running around cones, running backward, side to side and wonderfully crazy footwork. Oliver and George also watched the big guys' drills, mainly ramming flat bags and lifting weights.

The assistant coaches made the men do some plays to see how the quarterbacks threw and how the receivers caught the balls.

In addition to talent Oliver and George were looking for lightning-fast reactions. They wanted their minds to be as nimble as they bodies. They wanted them to be able to make quick decisions, as plays always changed without warning.

By the end of the tryouts Oliver and George compared notes and were pretty much on the same page. They sorted which players they would keep for the team, and of those which ones they liked for the offensive lines as well as the defensive ones, and the positions they believed they would be best at, even if the player originally played a different position.

Neil Howard was not among the players trying out.

Oliver kept him away on purpose. He didn't want any of the players trying out to be swayed by his presence. Everyone knew who Howard was, and his prowess as a player was appreciated, but his addiction pretty much killed his reputation and no one trusted him. Oliver needed to change that around and it would have to be done with finesse.

Two days later the players who tried out were summoned to the large conference room at the training facility. The coaches, assistants and staff were all present.

"Thank you all for coming to try out," Oliver said. "It has been a privilege meeting you and seeing your talent. The following names I call unfortunately did make it this year, but I would encourage you to keep trying. We have seen how much love you have for the game and you are amazing players. Don't give up. Should there be openings, and you are available, we definitely will contact you. Thank you again, gentlemen."

Oliver proceeded to read off the names. The cut players murmured their thanks and exited the room. The ones remaining, and many had sweat running down their spines, released the breath they had been holding for what seemed an eternity.

"Congratulations, gentlemen, it is an honor to have you as part of the newest team in the NFL—the New Mexico Natives!"

The players clapped and hollered. They were probably some of the happiest men on the planet.

"We, your coaches and staff including our owner, Mr. William Quinn, will try to do our best for you. We have no doubt you will do the same. You represent your team, yourselves, your families and even us. You are an achievement. You also represent sportsmanship, football, and most of all you, as men, are examples to youth about what your gender is made of. Show them what a man can be. Youngsters will look up to you and some may even be future professional football players because of you. You are of course rough, tough sons-of-bitches, and that's wonderful and part of your profession, but you are also the epitome of one of my favorite sayings from St. Francis de Sales: *'Nothing is so strong as gentleness, nothing so gentle as real strength'.*"

Oliver knew this was getting long and tedious, but he would only do this once and he needed the guys to understand what they and the team would be portraying. He continued: "In your personal life you need to be even better than you are on the field. I'm a pretty good judge of character and that is also one of the reasons you were chosen for this team. I don't believe that you would ever do unspeakable acts, such as violence of any kind, especially toward women, or road rage, just to name just a couple of examples. If you do, by the way, not only will you be expelled from this team, but I will make it my mission to make your life as miserable as possible. That would include not being able to play professional football, and most likely some jail time."

The players were getting bored, but they also heeded Oliver's words.

"Gentlemen, one last note. We are going to show the world that football is an art, like dancing or singing. It's also a passion, like cooking. And when you feel this about football there is grace." Oliver looked at the players who were just short of rolling their eyes toward the ceiling. "Especially when the ball is cradled in a player's arms and he flies into the end zone!"

"Yeah!" The players shouted in agreement.

"Are we clear, gentlemen?"

"Yes, Coach!"

"Alright, now head out to the bus. You'll be driven to meet with our owner, Mr. Quinn, who has a surprise for you."

"Yes, Coach!"

The new members of the New Mexico Natives were driven to the apartment complex. They filed out of the bus and headed inside. They waited as instructed in the lobby. William Quinn walked up to the front of the room where Oliver and the new players were standing.

"Okay, everybody," Oliver said. "We brought you here today to congratulate you once again for making the team. You are the very first players of the New Mexico Natives!" Everyone in the room clapped and hollered. "Also, you are getting the surprise which I mentioned, and our owner, Mr. William Quinn will tell you about it."

William looked at the men standing in front of him. He already was proud of the guys as he knew they were there because of the same burning desire he had. "Congratulations, gentlemen!" William said. "You are the newest NFL team and the first New Mexico Natives! We are going to embark on this venture together!"

The players clapped. They were excited, and it was reflected in the atmosphere.

"As Coach Hadley mentioned I have a surprise."

The new team members gave William their full attention. They knew the billionaire was a little eccentric, was filthy rich of course, but they had also heard that he was a cool guy and decent with his employees. They wondered what kind of surprise he had up his sleeve.

"As members of the Natives you will each get an apartment to use throughout the season, rent free and all utilities included. The other amenities, such as the pool and restaurant are available to you as well. This is all right here in this building, and this will make your commute to the training facility and to venues easier. These are just a couple of things you won't have to worry about and I believe the less concerns you have the more you can focus on the practices and the games."

The players were stunned and very grateful. They wouldn't have to search for accommodations and they would be living together, very much like a university dorm. They knew it would be a good atmosphere. They clapped and hollered their thanks.

"Good, I'm glad you approve. Now, I don't want anyone fighting over which apartment you get. The top two floors are reserved for myself and other staff members. The floors below will be everybody else. No discriminating, they're all the same." There was a table next to William with a basket. "Right now, I would like to shake each of your hands and give you a key."

Each player walked up to William, shook his hand and thanked him. Their new owner congratulated each one, pulled out a key indiscriminately from the basket and handed it to the new team member. It was Christmas in Spring and everyone was excited at what the upcoming weeks and months would bring.

CHAPTER 7  GRADUATION

Oliver Hadley and his staff had been hard at work for the last couple of months with the team. They were progressing nicely, but Oliver was looking forward to the next few days. It would be a nice diversion. He and William headed for the Citation X. Once on board the men sat in the plush seats and put their feet up.

"This is going to be a fun little break," Oliver said, "and best of all I get to see my little girl."

"I love Roberta as if she were my own. I'm sure you know this Oliver, but if anything should ever happen to you I don't want you to ever worry about her."

"Thanks, Will, I do know that."

The two men made themselves comfortable. It would be a long trip, although they had every convenience on board, from movies on a big screen they could watch together to individuals ones in their seats. There was a fully stocked bar and prepared hot meals in the galley oven. Of course they could also make themselves sandwiches with an array of exquisite charcuterie, cheeses and produce, either on a baguette or several other types of bread. Fresh fruit and pastries were ample as well.

William and Oliver enjoyed the conveniences and discussed the team. They were happy with the results so far, but they were also happy to be flying to England for Roberta's graduation.

The Citation X flew its passengers smoothly and in comfort to England. After landing at Oxford's airport William and Oliver were picked up and the limousine took them to one of the oldest universities in the world which dated back to 1096. They took in the sights of the historic city with its lovely parks, churches, gardens and of course the buildings of the University of Oxford.

Oliver and William walked toward the lovely Sheldonian Theater that had been built in 1665 and designed by Christopher Wren where the graduation would take place.

"You know, Oliver, what amazes me is that we are walking in the same streets that so many famous people before us have, and from all over the world. Remarkable men and women who attended this university who went on to become Nobel Prize winners, Monarchs, Prime Ministers, Presidents, Olympians, explorers, composers, authors, and the list goes on and on."

"You're right, and so many of our own U.S. cities and universities have names that came from this part of the world, especially in New England."

A few moments later Roberta ran up to her father and William. "Daddy! Uncle Will! I'm so glad you're here," she screamed as she hugged the two men she adored.

"Hi, sweetheart, you look absolutely stunning," Oliver said, seeing his daughter in her graduation gown. She looked so much like her mother. Diane would have been ridiculously happy seeing the exquisite, mature young woman their little girl had become.

"How is the most beautiful girl in the world?" William said, as he always had since she was little.

"Oh, Uncle Will, I'm really happy."

"Bravo, little one, and congratulations."

"Thank you. Uncle Will, Daddy, I would like you to meet Charles," Roberta said, introducing her boyfriend.

Oliver had spoken to him on the telephone and now he was finally meeting him face to face. He was a handsome young man and from their cross-Atlantic conversations he knew Charles was mature and had a good head on his shoulders. He also quickly noticed the look in his eyes when he looked at Roberta. They couldn't lie. He was in love with her, as was she with him. As a father he would have hoped she wouldn't date until she was at least forty, but in the present reality he wanted his daughter to be happy. She seemed to be just that. She wasn't his little girl anymore, rather she was a fine young woman and Oliver was truly happy for her and with her choice.

"Charles, nice to finally meet you," Oliver said sincerely as he shook the younger man's hand and grabbed his shoulder.

Charles did the same and said: "The pleasure is all mine." He turned to a woman standing behind him. "And my I introduce my sister, Lady Maxine Owen-Smith." The American man held his breath as he saw the stunning face. He also appreciated the lovely curves under the chic silk dark blue dress. Her strawberry blond hair was elegantly pulled back and her eyes were a unique shade of violet that the dress matched perfectly. He also wondered if her lips were as delicious as they looked. The ensemble was stunning.

"How do you do?" She asked Oliver.

"How do you do?" He repeated, without realizing that that was the appropriate English salutation. He had been taken aback by Lady Maxine and was grateful that at least a response came out of his mouth.

William followed suit. "How do you do?"

"Well, we have to run," Roberta announced. "We'll see you all after the ceremony."

"Okay, sweetheart. I'm very proud of you. Knock 'em dead."

Roberta and Charles headed out.

"Knock them dead? Who?" Maxine asked.

Oliver laughed. "It's an expression. It means really show them what you can do."

"I see. I was sure that Roberta wasn't just going to… oh, never mind. That girl couldn't kill a fly," she giggled.

Oliver, William and Maxine walked into the theater. It looked very much like an auditorium, one side with rounded walls, the other with straight ones. They found their seats and the Americans took in the theater that had seen ceremonies for centuries.

"The painting on the ceiling is exquisite," William remarked. As with many things he was an aficionado of the arts.

"Yes, it is rather lovely," Maxine agreed. It's by Robert Streater who was the court painter for King Charles II. The subject is truth descending upon the arts and sciences, banishing ignorance from the university," Maxine explained.

"That's very *à propos*, I like that. The theater is small but really nice," William commented.

"It is, and the acoustics are wonderful, however, be prepared for the ceremony, it's quite lengthy and the majority will be in Latin."

"Seriously?" William asked.

"Absolutely."

"And the seating is pretty hard on the… behind," Oliver added.

"You noticed," she said with a little smirk.

Oliver cocked his head. "How could I not? There isn't much padding back there."

Maxine chuckled. "I wish you courage."

"Thanks. You've known Roberta for a while?"

"Well, since she's been dating Charles. I must commend you Mr. Hadley, you've raised a magnificent young woman. You must be very proud."

"Thank you, that's kind of you, and yes, I am incredibly proud."

Maxine noticed a shadow forming over his eyes and she immediately understood. "I'm very sorry your wife could not be here, but I'm sure she has been watching over both of you ever since her tragic departure." Oliver looked at her. "Roberta told me so much about her, and you as well. All good things, of course." Maxine smiled.

"You're very kind, Lady Maxine."

"Oh, please, call me Max."

"If you call me Oliver."

"It's a deal."

"May I ask you a question?"

"Go right ahead."

"Do you think Roberta and Charles are serious, or is it just puppy love?"

"Well, I think they're more mature than a puppy love phase, and I've never seen Charles more taken by a young woman as he is now."

"You think so?"

"Oh, yes, and why wouldn't he be? She's absolutely lovely, extremely bright and has a good heart."

Oliver glowed with pride. "Thank you, that's very nice of you to say."

"I wouldn't say it unless I meant it."

"You know all that about her?"

"Oh, yes. She's been by the house many times with

Charles and I am a professor at one of the universities, which makes me somewhat of an authority on the young people around me."

Oliver was thinking she couldn't be over thirty. She had an easy way about her and he was sure her students enjoyed her classes. He was going to ask her what she taught, but he didn't get a chance.

"It looks like they're about ready to start." Maxine announced as the vice chancellor and other professors of the university came in, dressed in their own traditional caps and gowns.

The Vice Chancellor of Oxford University spoke for about fifteen minutes. Following the speech was the traditional ceremony spoken in Latin by the professors of their particular specialty such as medicine, philosophy, or mathematics and finally congratulated the graduates. Oliver knew they were speaking in Latin but their accents were so heavy they sounded as if they were speaking some incomprehensible form of English. The only thing he did understand was the names of the graduates or a Latin word that was used in English. When Roberta's name was announced Oliver wanted to scream and shout, instead he sat with wet eyes and was very quiet. He knew if he moved in any way he would lose it. The manly father completely melted away when it came to his little girl.

The ceremony lasted about an hour and a half with the graduates exiting the theater at some point and returning with the addition to their gown of a different scarf-like silk hood hanging down their backs and fronts. The color depended on their degrees. Roberta and Charles looked especially radiant with their own hoods draped over their shoulders.

When the ceremony was over they all went out to dinner. They had a lovely meal at an exquisite restaurant and learned a little more about each other.

"Well, I've been up for about thirty hours so I'm going to get some sleep," William announced.

"Yes, it has been quite a day," Roberta answered, "I think we're all a bit tired, albeit really happy! This has been one of the best days ever!" She hugged William and her father.

"It has been rather perfect," Oliver agreed, "and we're very proud of both of you."

"I'll second that," Maxine said.

They left the restaurant and said their goodnights, but Oliver looked at Maxine and suddenly the words spilled out of his mouth before he could stop them. "May I take you out to lunch or dinner tomorrow?"

"I'd like that. You can knock me up at seven," she answered.

Oliver's eyes nearly popped out of his sockets. "I'm sorry? What would you like me to do?"

"Pick me up at seven o'clock."

"Oh, sure, no problem," he said letting out the breath that had been stuck in his lungs.

Roberta and Charles, who had overheard, were practically in tears. Charles had done the same thing when the two of them had first met. When she understood the English expression she started laughing and thankfully hadn't slapped him. When she explained what the American version meant Charles was laughing so hard he was in tears.

"It's not far from town, but it's a little confusing. Ask a taxi driver to take you to the Owen-Smith Estate, they'll know," Maxine said to Oliver.

"Okay, I can do that."

They bade each other good night and went their separate ways.

As Oliver lay in bed in his hotel room he couldn't stop thinking about the exquisite Lady. Then he started laughing as he remembered she wanted to be knocked up at seven o'clock.

CHAPTER 8      FALLING COACH

The taxi drove Oliver out of Oxford and toward the Owen-Smith estate. It wasn't far and as soon as they cleared a forest Oliver saw a private road leading to the immense building looming in front of him. He opened his eyes wide as he stared. Hadn't Maxine called it a manor? He gawked at the imposing structure, a real English castle. It was beautiful, but he didn't feel very comfortable. He arrived promptly, as was his habit. He went up to the door and pulled the tongue of the lion-head door knocker. Moments later a classic older English butler opened the door. Oliver smiled and held back from calling him Jeeves. He so looked the part. "I'm Oliver…"

"Yes, Mr. Hadley, please follow me. Lady Maxine will join you in her office," said the perfectly groomed man, guiding him through a great hall adorned with ancient knights' armors and portraits of what surely were the Owen-Smith ancestors.

Oliver marveled at the enormous paintings on the great walls as he followed the butler until he was ushered into what looked like a library with an exquisite antique desk. The walls were adorned by beautifully handcrafted bookcases and the Persian carpets of wool and silk on the parquet floor were magnificent. The dark soft leather chairs and sofa were more masculine that he expected, but the flowers in the tall, exquisite Ming floor-to-window vases transformed the room with the graceful feminine touch he had anticipated. He scanned Maxine's books. It was a large collection of different genres, from elegant leather-bound classics of Dickens and the Brontës to modern popular fiction paperbacks. On one shelf, however, he noticed a series of books he thought rather unusual as he read the authors' names: Sun Tzu, Carl von Clausewitz, Subutai, Genghis Khan, Shivaji Maharaf, Alexander the Great, Hannibal, Napoleon, and Admiral Lord Nelson among many more. They all related to the art of war and military strategy.

Maxine entered her office. She was dressed casually in jeans and a sweater, and as Oliver checked her out he decided that even if she wore a loose burlap bag she would be stunning. The woman was just naturally elegant.

"Good evening, Oliver," she said, as her presence filled the room.

"You look lovely, Max."

"Thank you." So do you, she wanted to say. He did look rather delicious.

"I love your office. It's very nice."

"Thank you, I quite like it myself. It suits me and I'm comfortable in it. It's a good place to think and work."

"It sounds like you're happy with what you do," Oliver said.

"Oh, I am. There isn't anything quite like a young mind who wants to learn and discover, and I am delighted when I can add to their edification. But I must confess, right now I'm famished. We can continue our conversation in a moment. Shall we get going first?"

"Absolutely. Is there a certain restaurant you would prefer?" Oliver asked, not knowing where to take this lady to dinner.

"Well, since I know the eateries around here and you probably don't, how about if I take you to a quaint little pub with great food."

Oliver was thrilled. He hadn't been in a mood for an elegant restaurant and a pub sounded good and probably fun. "Perfect."

"Great, let's go. We'll take the car, and I'll drive, wrong side of the road and all that to you."

"Okay," he chuckled.

Maxine drove into Oxford and parked in front of a local pub. The building was old. Oliver estimated it must have been around for at least a century, maybe two. He opened the heavy wooden door for Maxine and followed her in. He smiled as he stepped into history—massive wooden beams hung from the low ceiling, the walls were covered with faded 19th century horses and buggies wallpaper, the Union Jack was proudly featured on one of the walls and the long shiny polished wooden bar went from one end of the room to the other. On the wall behind the bar prominent bottles of whiskey and over a dozen assorted tap handles were proudly displayed awaiting the customer's preference. Somewhat more modern was a pool table in one corner and of course the beloved dart board with men trying to outdo one another with their small arrows. Although it was somewhat dark it was just the right lighting and the pub welcomed its patrons for an evening they would hopefully enjoy.

"Good evenin' to you, Lady Maxine," the man behind the bar said.

"Good evening Gerald," she answered back with a delightful smile.

"You havin' your usual?"

"Most probable, but let me see what my friend would like. I'll let you know in a few minutes."

Maxine and Oliver sat down at a table in a corner of the pub.

"This is quite the place," Oliver said, enthused by the typicality of the tavern.

"This is your quintessential English pub, with the hearth in one corner keeping the patrons warm just as it has for over a hundred and fifty years."

"It's really great. They've been going for that long, huh?"

"They have."

"What's their secret?"

"Good beer, good food, good service and repeat customers."

"All good," Oliver said and they both laughed.

"Hungry?" Maxine asked.

"Famished. Is there a menu?"

"Look up there and you'll see it. It's the slate board."

Oliver looked up and saw a chalkboard. It read:

Sunday Roast
Bubble and Squeak
Bangers and Mash
Spotted Dick

"It's the standard menu. It never changes," Maxine said.

"That's convenient."

"It is. Simple and tasty."

Oliver was studying the board and said: "You might have to help me and translate a couple of the items on the menu."

"Certainly."

"Sunday roast I presume is some sort of meat with potatoes and vegetables."

"That's right, and comes with Yorkshire pudding."

"Pudding?"

Maxine giggled. "Think of it as the bread of the meal, but more like an individual mini dough soufflé."

"That sounds good."

"Delicious actually, and accompanies a very English traditional meal. That's what I'm ordering."

"Okay, me too."

Maxine turned to the man at the bar and held up two fingers. He nodded and gave her a thumbs up.

Oliver watched and then said. "That was the order, wasn't it?"

"It was. That's what I always get, although every once in a while I'll get the bangers and mash."

"I presume those are sausages and mashed potatoes."

"That's right."

"Why are they called bangers?" Oliver asked. He didn't want to think of anything sexual, although with the beauty sitting across from him, it was pretty difficult.

"During WWI there was a meat shortage and they would fatten the sausages with water. When they cooked they would burst."

"Interesting. And Bubble and Squeak? This meal probably doesn't explode, and when it is cooking I could see how it could bubble. But how does it squeak?"

Maxine chuckled. "You're right. It's a dish of mash with leftover vegetables. One grills it until golden brown and because there is cabbage inside it squeaks when it cooks."

"No kidding?"

"No kidding," Maxine repeated.

"Okay, this last one scares me."

Maxine laughed. "I'm sure it does."

"Dare I ask what Spotted Dick is?"

"I'll tell you."

Oliver raised an eyebrow. "I'm listening."

"Dick is an old word for pudding."

"Yes, Professor."

"Spotted Dick is a kind of steamed, hot sponge cake with raisins, served with custard."

Oliver wondered if it also had nuts.

One of the students, who clearly had consumed one too many pints of the local ale, stumbled up to Maxine's table. Two of his buddies, who weren't far behind him as far as beers, tried their best to hold him steady. The young man stood at attention as best he could and saluted her. "Professor, I'm Peter Stanley and I'm one of your students," he slurred.

"Yes, I know who you are, Mr. Stanley," Maxine said with a gracious smile. She knew the students studied hard and unwinding every once in while was practically a requirement, as long as they didn't go too far.

"I just wanted to... profess to you that all professors should uh... profess like you," he said. "Just wanted to... profess that to you, and to thank you for all you've done for me and all of your students. I, we, well, all of us really...," he said as he threw his arms in the direction of his friends around the room. The two who were holding him up ducked just in time. They also immediately nodded and agreed. Stanley continued: "we all... profess that you are our favorite... professor, Professor."

"Hear! Hear!" The patrons who had been watching in the filled pub shouted. They were mainly students, some family members and the regulars. They were witnessing the bond of the student with his teacher, but certainly believed this was not his normal behavior in class and probably would never have the wherewithal to tell his mentor when he was sober. They wondered how the professor would respond.

"Thank you, Mr. Stanley. I... *profess* that's very kind, and I also *profess* that I'm very fond of you." She looked around and continued to the crowd, "as I am of all my students here."

The crowd roared. Not only did she confirm she liked them, the Lady had a sense of humor too.

Oliver watched the tête-à-tête and thought Stanley might be infatuated with his mentor, something most boys with good-looking teachers experienced. He couldn't fault the young man who really did have a beautiful professor, and if Oliver had had a teacher like Maxine he would surely have felt the same way.

Stanley's buddies took him away to their table.

"That was nice to see," Oliver said.

"Oh, they're a fun lot. I know how hard they study all through the year and getting positive feedback is always pleasant."

"And I have a feeling that they have a wonderful teacher and put a little extra effort in to please her."

"That's kind of you to say."

"Well I certainly would if you if I were in your class."

"Thank you, Oliver."

"Oh, I mean it." If only you knew how much, Oliver thought.

Their meal arrived and they both thoroughly enjoyed it.

"Now, Charles is your younger brother, right?" Oliver asked, making small talk in order to get his mind off those lips he was dying to touch. He watched them open and close with every one of the morsels she put in her mouth. Oh, how he longed to be one of those pieces.

"That's right. My brother Richard is the oldest and Lord of the castle. I'm in the middle and Charles is the baby. It seems my parents had a child every ten years. We're now forty-two, thirty-two for me, and Charles is twenty-two."

"Does everyone live in the castle?"

"Richard and his wife and two boys do. He also runs it. I have what I call an apartment, which is actually one wing of the castle with my own living room or entertainment room, a bedroom, a guest room and my office. Charles has a wing as well, but prefers to stay at university. The estate is so big that we could go on for weeks without seeing each other, but it works out well for everybody and we're all happy with our lives."

"Sounds really nice. Did you always want to be a teacher?"

"No, actually when I was young I wanted to be a veterinarian. I wanted to save animals, but then I loved sports and I wanted to be on the Olympic equestrian team, to compete in combination dressage, jumping and cross country. But then when I went to college I wanted to be an archeologist. I was fascinated by history and the ancient world, and I wanted to discover what hadn't yet been discovered. That led me to my love of the art of war and military strategy."

"I noticed quite a few books in your office. How did you wind up loving that? That's usually pretty brutal," Oliver wondered as he asked.

"That's true, however, and I don't particularly like that aspect of it, but I very much appreciate the art of it. The strategy of how the military minds play their game."

"Their game?"

"Yes, like chess. They had to be incredibly precise and very creative. Those generals had to outwit, outmaneuver and outsmart the enemy. The more they were underdogs, the more innovative they became."

Oliver was fascinated by everything Maxine was saying, but he was more enthused by the stunning woman across from him. "Why didn't you join the military? It sounds like you might have enjoyed it."

"I thought about it, and it would have been the logical choice, but I don't like taking orders, and with a black belt in Aikido I could picture myself giving the male dominated profession a lesson or two. I don't think I would have lasted very long."

Oliver laughed. "I quite understand, but their loss, though."

"Absolutely." Maxine took a sip of her beer.

She's got a black belt in martial arts! Appropriate with her studies, Oliver thought. He watched her lips straddle the rim of her glass and his manhood immediately reacted. He wanted her, oh, how he wanted her. He hadn't felt this way about a woman since Diane. It was the first time he was interested, really interested. And yes, he wanted to discover every inch of her, every curve, every sensual zone, and he wanted to please her.

"Alright, enough about me, what about you? Tell me about yourself," Maxine said, pulling him back from his reverie.

Oliver did. The two of them spoke for a couple more hours while they nursed their beers. The man had opened up and spoken about his life that had been dormant for many years. It was the first time since his wife had died that he was comfortable with another human being, especially a woman.

When they left the restaurant Maxine drove Oliver to his hotel. Before leaving the car he turned to her and said: "May I kiss you?"

Maxine looked at him and smiled as she nodded.

Oliver leaned forward and gently touched his lips to hers. Damn! He'd been right. They were as delicious as he had imagined. Maxine responded with more ardor than either one of them anticipated. Her arms wrapped around his neck and he held her close to him. He would have loved if she came up to his room, but he didn't want to seem too pushy. He decided to take it slow and not ruin the beginning of something possibly very special. He slowly got out of the car and said: "May I knock you up tomorrow?"

"I would love that," she answered.

The next morning Oliver and William were eating breakfast in the hotel restaurant when Roberta showed up.

"Good morning you two. What are you eating? I'm starving!" She announced, sitting at the table.

"But you ate last night," William teased.

"Oh, Uncle Will, I can eat any of your linebackers under the table."

"That she could," Oliver agreed.

"What's your secret, little one?" William asked.

"Eat anything you want, be happy, oh, and exercise," she grinned.

"Of course."

Oliver's mind had been wandering, his thoughts on Maxine. "Robbie, why isn't Maxine married?" He unexpectedly asked his daughter.

William smiled. He knew it. Coach Oliver was falling for the English woman.

Roberta giggled. "The lady has high standards, Dad," she answered. "But you would definitely measure up," she added quickly.

"I would? Ah, you're biased."

"Of course I am, but I also speak the truth. I really like her, and it's time, Dad. I'm sure, no, I *know* Mom would want you to be happy." Roberta knew that he liked Maxine and probably had some guilty feelings about not being loyal to her mother. Her father was only thirty-eight years old and she really wanted him to have companionship. He was too young to be alone and deserved a second chance at a relationship and perhaps even love. If the Lady was the one slowly invading his heart she was thrilled at the prospect.

Oliver looked at his lovely, mature daughter. When had she grown up? When had she become such an amazing young woman? What happened to the little girl who ran up to her Daddy, the rock who would protect her from everything, the one she would throw her little arms around his neck and squeeze so tight? They would always be father and daughter, but now they were also best friends and could confide in one another as adults. He knew it was impossible to love her any more than he already did, but he could swear that each day his infinite fountain of love for her gushed even more. He looked into her soft hazel eyes and asked: "You wouldn't mind if things maybe got serious, sweetheart?"

"Of course not, Daddy. On the contrary, you deserve to be happy and if Maxine is your choice I couldn't agree more. I absolutely love her as a person, she's one hell of a teacher and she has a title, which is fun as well. And let's not forget what a knockout she is!"

"I hadn't noticed."

"Daddy!"

"You're so full of it, Hadley," William chuckled.

"Yeah? You really wouldn't mind, sweetheart?" Oliver asked her again, wanting to be really sure.

Roberta jumped up and hugged her father. "Go for it, Daddy, and cradle her like your favorite football."

William laughed. "Now *that* he understands."

Oliver returned his daughter's embrace.

A few minutes later the stunning Lady Maxine Owen-Smith was walking toward them. Her younger brother Charles next to her, his eyes riveted on Roberta.

CHAPTER 9  COACH'S TOUCHDOWN

A Few minutes later the stunning Lady Maxine Owen-Smith was walking toward them. Her younger brother Charles next to her, his eyes riveted on Roberta.

"Good morning, Max, Charles." William said as he and Oliver immediately stood up.

"Good morning," they both answered.

"Have you had breakfast?" Roberta asked.

"Yes, we have, thank you."

"I have to make a quick trip to Paris. What do you all have planned for today?" William asked.

"Charles and I are going to take it easy," Roberta said, "walk around the town a little and maybe just lay in the park all day long. The weather is absolutely perfect."

"That it is," Maxine said, "sounds like a wonderful plan. I was thinking I could drive Oliver around the countryside and see the sights. There are lovely little villages in these parts."

"Well, I guess everyone is doing something fun," Oliver said. "You two enjoy," he said to Roberta and Charles, "and you too, Will. Paris won't be the same once you get there."

"Oh, it will be, not to worry, the City of Light never changes."

"Oliver? Are you ready to head out?" Maxine said.

"Let's go," he said. The man was as excited as a school boy on his first date.

They bade each other goodbye and went their separate ways.

Maxine and Oliver were almost at the car when he realized he'd forgotten his wallet. "Oh, Max, I forgot my wallet in the room. Let me just run up and get it."

"That's fine," she answered. She looked at the man for a moment and then said: "Oliver, you know, this is silly of me and I should have thought of it sooner, but I really need to use the washroom. Would it be an imposition if I used the one in your room?"

"Of course not."

They went back into the hotel and up to Oliver's room. As soon as he closed the door Maxine pinned him against it and kissed him hard. The man didn't need any more coaxing and responded in kind. When they came up for a breath he picked her up and headed for the bedroom. She put her arms around his neck and kissed him again. He put her on the bed and looked at her. She was exquisite and he couldn't wait to please her.

"Oliver."

"Yes, Max, is everything alright?"

"I just want you to know that I appreciate how much of a gentleman you were last night, but it drove me crazy and I practically didn't sleep."

Oliver grinned. "I didn't either."

"I don't usually act like this, but it seems just so right with you."

"I know what you mean," Oliver said, and gently kissed her lips.

There was anticipation, there was lust, there was discovery, and there was beautiful harmonious love making. They learned each other's bodies, kissed and caressed the most sensitive regions, uncovered the little secrets that gave the other exquisite pleasure. They respected and enjoyed the emotions they were passionately sharing and giving each other. They flawlessly melted together until they culminated into their euphoric enchantment.

Oliver and Maxine spent the rest of the day making love, ordering room service and watching television.

When Oliver woke up the next morning his shoulder slightly throbbed. When he tried to move it he realized that Maxine was the reason. She had snuggled up to him and had fallen asleep. He smiled and forgot the ache. It had been so long since he wanted to wake up with a woman in his arms. He was glad it was Maxine. He looked at her peaceful face and marveled at the stunning features of what the locals lovingly called the epitome of their beautiful women, an English rose. He wanted to keep staring at her and hold her for hours, but he couldn't resist and gently caressed the beguiling face. Her lips curved into a smile and she opened her eyes.

"Good morning, Oli," she purred.

"I didn't mean to wake you."

"No worries. I found it rather lovely waking up like that."

"I'm glad," Oliver said.

"What would you like to do today?" She asked. "Would you like to take a drive? There are some marvelous little towns all around here," she giggled, thinking about how she had said something similar the previous day.

"That sounds nice," he said slowly.

"Or we could just stay in and order room service," Maxine said sensually as she inched on top of him.

"Now you're talking, Lady Maxine," Oliver agreed as he passionately kissed her soft, luscious lips and pulled her closer to him.

Oliver and Maxine stayed in the hotel room for the rest of the day. They made love several times and then ordered room service. They decided to stay in and watch an American football game. Oliver hoped she would enjoy it. Maxine didn't seem too enthused, but was a perfect lady and went along.

When the food arrived it consisted of bangers, chips and ale, the English version of hot dogs, French fries and beer. Oliver wanted to give Maxine as much of 'the full experience' as possible without physically being at a stadium. They watched a game on YouTube.

While they enjoyed their meal Maxine seemed a little bored. Never having been to an American football game or watched it on television she was a bit lost. Oliver picked up on it and started to explain.

Of course Maxine had a hundred questions. Her very first one was: "Why is it called *foot*ball? They don't do anything to the ball with their feet."

"Football, the world-wide version that is played around the world and what we Americans call soccer was the forerunner of today's American football. When they decided they wanted to use hands the game became 'rugby football', kind of a combination of both. Rugby took on world-wide appeal. The Americans loved this new game, changed and added a few rules, formed a game as it is known today and retained the name but took out 'rugby'. That's how the name and the game came to be. It's the country's national sport. Now, why they didn't just dream up another word at the time is beyond me. It would have made more sense to name it something else, maybe something more American."

Maxine saw 'WR' next to a player's name. "The 'WR' stands for world record?"

"Wide receiver," he answered.

"Oh," she giggled at her own ignorance.

Oliver thought it was completely endearing. It also told him that she was a sports aficionado and an athlete herself.

Confusing to Maxine was the way the players 'piled up'.

"Why don't they just pass the ball instead of making a mini-mountain on top of the player that has the ball, who probably feels he's being squashed like a cockroach?"

Oliver laughed and tried to explain the 'first and ten' concept and they were trying to pick up some crucial yards. Maxine was starting to understand more of the tactics and rules of the game. He explained each player's role on the offense and defense, the special teams and the scoring.

As they watched some more something suddenly 'clicked' and Maxine started hollering at the TV: "Oh, my God, Oliver, I got it! They only need two yards! Do a pile-up! Do the pile-up thing!"

The man watched the beautiful woman and laughed hard. "I see you're understanding more and more, and really getting into the game."

"Oh, yes, now that I'm understanding it better, it's really fun. It's very strategic."

"Yeah?"

"Absolutely."

They watched some more and of course Maxine had another question: "Why, when the rules are so picky about both feet being placed exactly in the end zone is it okay to dive over players with just the ball crossing the line, whether their bodies do or don't, is it considered a touchdown? Or when the players just fly past the pylon can they score?" This really didn't make any sense to Maxine.

Oliver laughed and he would explain more as they watched.

"The one that throws, what's the name, he picks which player to throw it to?

"The quarterback?"

"Yes, him. Does he throw it to whoever's open?"

"That's the idea, but it's more strategic than that."

"Really?" Maxine asked, her interest peaking a little more.

"Yes, we have what we call a playbook."

"Sounds like music."

"It's kind of like an orchestra. The maestro, that would be me, the coach, dreams up plays which we practice *ad nauseam*. A playbook is a compilation of many, many, many plays."

"Now there's a handsome guy," Maxine pointed to the man waiting for the snap.

"Ah, that my dear is Tom Brady, one of the best quarterbacks the game has ever had, also known as the GOAT."

"A goat? What do you mean?" Maxine asked, confused.

"Greatest Of All Time."

"Ah, G.O.A.T., got it. Who came up with that?"

"LL Cool J, if I'm not mistaken."

"The rapper and actor?"

"I'm pretty sure, though I think he credits Muhammad Ali."

"I like both of them, and Tommy too of course."

Maxine focused back on the game and watched the quarterback as he put his hands up to his center in front of him.

"Is he putting his hands under his bum…?" Maxine trailed off.

Oliver roared. "Yes, he is. A center to quarterback relationship is very special. A lot of trust on both sides. The quarterback has to put just the right pressure on his butt, so that the center knows he's there and ready to catch the ball. In turn the center has to give his quarterback the ball perfectly, the laces exactly placed where needed and the ball right into the perfect position of the quarterback's hand. The height of the butt is also important."

Maxine listened attentively, trying very hard not to laugh as Oliver explained the details. The coach continued: "The players in the last position of the offensive line, one on the right and one on the left, are called tight ends," Oliver said.

"Oh, yes they are," Maxine agreed watching the players taking off and running down the field. "Oh, my word, this is getting sexier by the minute… Really tight uniforms, players grabbing each other, hands placed in very unusual places…"

"Lady Maxine Owen-Smith!" Oliver exclaimed in mock shock.

"What's wrong, big boy?" She said sensually, "after what we've…" Maxine didn't finish her sentence with words but with fingers all over his face and torso. Before she had time to continue Oliver stopped the game, picked her up and carried her to the bedroom.

"Do you know that back in the old days the quarterback would scratch the center's leg as a signal for him to snap the ball?"

"I never realized how sexy this American football really is!"

"And of course, the coach is the playmaker," Oliver grinned.

"Would you show me some of your plays, Coach?" Maxine asked sensually.

"It would be my pleasure."

When they resumed watching the game they enjoyed a pizza room service had provided. Maxine of course had more questions.

"Why does the quarterback say 'hut'? Sounds like a military order that drill sergeants have used since World War II, from 'Attention!'"

"It originally started out as 'hike' and then got shortened to 'hut' and I believe you're right, it is derived from the military commands such as 'attention!' Football and marching bands use it for their formations. When the quarterback says it that is the signal for the center to snap the ball to him."

"And what are they watching on those iPads? Plays? Doesn't the coach do that?" She asked.

"Yes, they refresh themselves of the plays. Also, do you see the little green dot on the back of the quarterback's helmet?"

"I do."

"There's also one on the defense's team."

"What does it mean?"

"That there is a speaker inside and they can hear what their coach has to say, although they can't speak back."

"How interesting," Maxine said, and really meant it. "So a coach tells them what play to do. Do the players always follow the play?"

"Usually, but if they don't that's an audible."

"As in an audiobook from Amazon?" What was he talking about?

"No, an audible is a change of play by the quarterback after the coach has told him a different play."

"You know, in a different century football coaches would have been brilliant generals and strategists."

"I can see that, and I thank you for the compliment. Does this mean you would then be my Josephine?" Oliver asked. Would the two of them become similar to the epic romance? He hoped she would say yes.

"I believe, my brilliant general, that you already are my Napoleon."

Oliver paused the game again and reached out to her. She slid into his arms and they sensually rediscovered more of each other's bodies.

Football games usually lasted about three hours. The one they had been watching was paused so many times that it took most of the day to get through it.

The next morning Oliver carefully left the bed as not to wake Maxine up. He went to the bathroom and took a shower. When he finished he tied a towel around his waist. He looked at the mirror over the sink and the face staring back at him, and noticed a difference—he looked happier than he had in years. He thought of his lady, their passionate love making and smiled. He threw his arms up in the air and jumped as if he were a player having just scored. He internally hollered TOUCHDOWN! The towel from his waist dropped to the floor. He looked at the spot where the towel had been and chuckled. "You're a happy boy too, aren't you?"

Oliver picked up his phone in the bathroom and called William who immediately answered.

"Hey Will, I have a favor to ask."

"What's up?"

"I'd like to stay a couple more days. Can we do that? I can ask George and the other coaches to take over until we get back." William didn't answer. He was waiting for Oliver to give him some sort of explanation and then it 'clicked' as his best friend rambled on. "Don't you have to something more to do in Paris, or London or Stockholm?"

"Why you ol' devil! You've really fallen for Max, haven't you?" William was thrilled. Oliver deserved some happiness in the love department.

Oliver stared blankly. "How do you know? Uh, you think so?"

"You know better than I do, but to be honest I've been watching the glow in your eyes get brighter every time you see that lovely lady. Go for it Oliver. Whether it's one day, a whirlwind fling or perhaps even years. You've nothing to lose and everything to gain. Give that heart of yours a new smile."

Oliver's lips curled up. "Yeah?"

"Yeah," William repeated. "We'll stay a couple more days. I'll find something to keep me occupied."

"I have no doubt. Thanks, Bro," Oliver said and hung up. He headed back to Lady Maxine.

William hung out in Paris with good friends and enjoyed great food and exquisite parties.

Oliver and Maxine had dinner that evening at their favorite pub, sitting side by side, enjoying their 'usual'— the Sunday Roast. Oliver was still weary of the Spotted Dick and didn't order desert. They didn't stay too long and once finished headed to the hotel.

How was he going to leave her behind? Oliver kept asking himself how it was possible to have fallen in love so fast. The more he thought about leaving the more he understood how hard he had fallen for Maxine. Was it the expression that said 'you know at first sight'? He had, hadn't he? As they walked hand in hand down the streets of the old city Oliver stopped and faced her. "Max!" He almost shouted. An idea had just formed in his mind and he hoped it would be the solution to his dilemma.

"What is it?" She asked, almost worried.

"You're off from the university for the summer, right?"

"Right."

"I have an idea. Hear me through and I hope you'll give me answer, well, the one I would like."

"Alright, I'm listening."

"We've spent an amazing time together."

"Yes, we have," Maxine agreed, suddenly worried that this man was now going to break her heart.

"After Diane died I thought my life had ended as well. I was sure I would never find another woman I would want to share my life with. I didn't even want to have a relationship, let along get serious with someone. Thankfully I had Roberta and she kept me going." Oliver stopped for a moment to caress her cheek, but he continued, worried that he wouldn't be able to finish. "You and Diane are completely different. I loved her with all my heart and she will always be a piece of my history. But love is amazing, it's infinite, and when you entered into my life all of a sudden I began to live again. You made me want to be the best man I can be, most especially to you, a stunning woman. I want to please you, to spend endless hours, days and months on end with you. Oh, Max, you've reopened my soul. I want you to know how very special you are to me."

Maxine looked at the man she had fallen in love with as well, and did her very best to keep the tears from falling from her eyes.

"Max," he continued, "I want to thank you, and I want you to be sure of this infinite love I have for you as well."

Maxine hugged Oliver and finally let the tears run down her cheeks. They embraced for a long while and then Oliver said: "Would you fly back with us to New Mexico tomorrow? I don't want to be anywhere without you. You could spend the summer there. We would be together for as long as we wanted." He looked into the exquisite violet of her eyes. What would be her answer, he wondered.

Maxine looked at the handsome face and cupped it in her hands. "Oli, I want you to know that I love you very, very much. I have never loved a man like I love you, and I have no doubt whatsoever that I will always love you." She lowered her hands from his face and took his into hers. "I want you to always remember how much you loved Diane. That will never bother me, on the contrary that just shows me how deeply you know how to love and that is one of the things I adore about you." She smiled at her man.

Oliver stared at the shiny eyes, hoping she would say yes and not break his heart.

"That sounds absolutely lovely! Yes, oh, yes! I have nothing planned for a few weeks and I would love to visit New Mexico."

"Really? You would?" Oliver asked incredulously. *How had that been so damn easy? The woman could make up her mind, and fast!* Yet one more thing he liked about her.

"Yes, really. I would love to! I just have to make a few calls, pack some clothes and grab my laptop and my passport," she said excitedly and then briefly slowed her pace. "This sounds amazing, Oli, and I just happen to know this guy who's the most phenomenal lover in the world."

Oliver raised an eyebrow. "Really?"

"Uh, huh," Maxine said as she moved closer to him.

"I think I just might know this guy, and I am sure he is very eager to please his lady," Oliver said, and kissed her passionately under the antique light of the ancient city.

CHAPTER 10  PRACTICE

On the flight over from England Maxine had opened her laptop and researched everything she could on American football. It was as if she had been bitten by the football bug. Now that she understood the basics, and perhaps even more thanks to Oliver's responses to all her questions, she became more and more infatuated. She was almost sad when the plane was ready to land after the long flight as she wanted to continue, but she closed her computer and marveled at the landscape on their approach over Albuquerque. She watched as the tan desert merged with the Sandia Mountains which were turning red from the sunset. It was unlike anything she had ever seen, and certainly wasn't the green canvas of the forests and plains of England.

After landing William, Oliver, Maxine and Captain Scott were picked up and driven to the apartment complex. William couldn't wait to see Dezba and quickly bade his fellow travelers a good night. Oliver showed Maxine his apartment. She was particular appreciative of the view. They hadn't slept on the plane so they wouldn't be jetlagged and went to bed early. They would be ready for the next day's practice.

The next morning Maxine and Oliver went to the training facility. Neither one wanted to leave each other's side and were constantly together. The coach went out to the field. She watched attentively from the sidelines as her man directed his players and staff. He definitely was a maestro of his profession and she also noticed how much respect everyone gave him. That evening, back at the apartment, Maxine wanted to help in any way she could so she asked Oliver: "May I make some suggestions for the warm-up?"

"Sure, what did you have in mind?"

"I could show the players some exercises that are used in Aikido. I think it would be beneficial in areas such as flexibility, mental strength and most importantly in avoiding injuries."

"I like the sound of that. Can you show me what you have in mind?"

"Of course." Maxine stood in the middle of the living room and showed Oliver the moves and exercises. As always the lady impressed him, especially when she did a move he never saw coming and landed with his back on the carpet. He looked up at her and raised an eyebrow.

"Would that be considered a penalty?" She asked.

"Uh, huh."

"Well, we'll just tweak it a little. We wouldn't want to get caught and lose yards," Maxine said sensually as she lowered herself over Oliver and kissed him passionately. He immediately responded and they forgot about martial arts and concentrated on each other.

In the morning Oliver introduced Maxine to the players. "Guys, this is Lady Maxine Owen-Smith. She is a good friend of the Natives and is going to help you out with some slightly different exercises stemming from

Aikido. She has a black belt and I will ask you to give her your undivided attention. Oh, and for pity's sake don't underestimate her."

"Yes, Coach!"

Oliver turned to Maxine. "They're all yours, Max."

"Thank you, Oli." She turned to the players. "Gentlemen, call me Max and would you please line up as if you were doing jumping jacks." They did as she asked. "You have already done some stretching exercises and now you're going to do *ukemi*, which translates from the Japanese as 'break falls'. Aikido is a martial art but its focus is not in the offense, such as hitting an opponent, rather it is an energy that connects between two people. Once you understand this it will help you figure out what the opposing player is about to do. In addition, this exercise helps to avoid injuries and get you out of tight spots. The ultimate goal is that your mind and body will have the movements stored subconsciously as muscle memory. Let's begin."

Maxine waved one of the men over who was of course much bigger than she was. The players chuckled at the ridiculous difference in sizes until she asked the linebacker to push her as if she were an opposing player. He did as she asked, albeit gently, and before he knew what she was doing he found himself on the ground in a split-second. The others laughed. Oliver grinned, not only because of what just happened to the big man but also because he remembered he had been in the same predicament as the player on the grass the night before. Of course he loved the way Maxine had followed-up with their own unique version.

Maxine explained to the men, who were now completely attentive to her clarification, that the move was a defensive one and that it had to be performed correctly or it could be considered a penalty. The players took an immediate liking to her and she showed them the move in slow motion. She used the big man again. He was ready for another slam. The other players laughed as they saw a hint of apprehension in his eyes. What would Max do to him now? They could hardly wait but Maxine didn't throw him around like a puppet, rather she showed them more movements.

"Please partner up and face each other." She was a good teacher and they quickly learned not only that particular move but several more. Maxine's training was aimed at helping the players be more in tune with their bodies and aware of their coordination, as well as improve power of specific muscles.

Maxine and the players did Aikido exercises for another half an hour. When she and Oliver were satisfied the members of the new team went to other coaches for their particular drills.

Neil Howard went down the field and practiced with his receivers. Oliver, Maxine and George watched as the QB threw some nice clean spirals to them.

"He's really smooth, isn't he?" Maxine said, impressed by the way Neil was placing the ball exactly where the receivers needed.

"Yes, he is. Neil could be our very own Drew Brees or Tom Brady," Oliver answered. "He is pretty amazing. Great arm and instincts."

"Football can really be graceful," Maxine added. It was a pleasure watching perfection and Neil was definitely providing that with each throw.

"Do you think he'll keep clean?" George asked.

"I hope so. For the moment I haven't seen or heard anything to the contrary. I know he's trying hard."

"Let's pray it stays that way."

"Alright, George, why don't you go take over with the QBs. I want to talk to some of the other guys.

Oliver had the offensive line practice some sweeps and pitchouts, mainly lateral passes from the back receiving the snap from the center to another back behind the line of scrimmage. They also practiced some plays with a few buttonhooks or digs where the receivers ran toward the end zone, stopped hard, caught the ball and ran down the field.

The coaches worked the players hard. They learned the plays, not that many, but they rehearsed them over and over until everyone was sure they would dream about them in their sleep. Some of the plays had come from Maxine's mind and the members of the Natives were amazed by how inventive they were. They couldn't wait to try them out in their first game of the season and see the results.

CHAPTER 11  ASSISTANT TO THE COACH

Oliver and Maxine were at the apartment. They were going to have a quiet evening dining on pizza and some nice wine while they talked about football. Once Maxine had understood the strategies she had become enthralled with the game. Oliver watched the woman he had fallen hard for. He especially loved the combination of brains and beauty. And what red-blooded American man who loved football didn't appreciate talking about details of the sport with his magnificent lover?

"Oli, its ready, take a seat," Maxine said as she carried the pizza to the table.

"Great, I'm famished." He walked to the counter and poured them each a glass of wine and brought it to the table. He sat down and Maxine placed pieces of the pie on the plates in front of them. They immediately started eating and enjoyed their dinner.

"Oli, I have some plays I've been working on."

"Oh?"

"Yes, but as you know, I'm not always sure if some things are allowed. Some of the rules are still confusing to me."

"Don't feel bad. Very few people understand everything."

"Would you look at them?"

"Sure. What've you got?"

Maxine went to get a notebook and opened it. She laid it on the table and showed him her first drawing. She explained the play and drew lines from Xs on the paper to other Xs. "What do you think? Are there rules against this?" Oliver did not answer, rather his face was frozen. "Oli, are you okay? Is something wrong?"

"Max, this is… totally… off the wall," he said gently.

"Oh." She simply said. She had hoped he would have liked the play. She lowered her eyes, a little embarrassed that she thought she, a brilliant military strategist, could have somehow helped the team.

Oliver grinned. "This is totally brilliant! We're going to try this out and it will be called the Max Special!"

"Really?"

"Absolutely! Oh, my, do you have more crazy plays like this?"

"Uh, huh, quite a few," she answered, elated by his reaction.

"Well, let's check these out!"

They continued for hours, unaware of how much time passed. When they were finally tired Oliver turned to her. "Max, I have two questions for you."

"You do?"

"Yes."

"And they are?"

"Would you live here with me, and would you be my assistant as well?"

"How do you mean?

"On the field, with the team, by my side."

"Seriously?"

"Totally." Oliver looked deep into her eyes.

"For how long?"

"I know you usually start school after summer, but

could you maybe take off longer? A few months until the season is over? Like a sabbatical?"

"You've been thinking about this for a while, haven't you?"

"I have, my love."

The next day after practice Maxine followed Oliver into the locker room. Two men working in the hallway noticed.

"Did that woman just go into the players' locker room?" The younger of the two asked.

"Uh, huh," the older man grunted.

"Have you seen her before?"

"Uh, huh." The older man repeated. He didn't speak too much. His co-worker did most of the talking, to his great annoyance.

"Is she a stripper or something? She's really hot."

"No, idiot, that's Lady Maxine," he grumbled.

"That's a good name for a dancer." The younger man said, satisfied and continued working.

"She's Coach Hadley's gal." The older man rolled his eyes and kept working.

"Oh, okay."

The players were standing in the room. They had just showered and were covered by a towel around their waists. Oliver looked at his team. He was proud of them. They had worked hard and were devoted to the Natives and to the game. Maxine stood next to him as he made his announcement: "Gentlemen, I am pleased to announce that we have an additional assistant coach." The players waited. Oliver motioned to Maxine. "Here she is."

The men clapped dutifully. They liked her, she was a great help with the unusual exercises and they knew she was a strategist and helped out with plays, but she was a girl. They wondered if that would be a problem.

Maxine understood their awkwardness as they stood there dressed in just their towels. She tried to put them at ease. "Look guys, I'm European, and our philosophy is simple. Everyone has a body. One is male, one is female. We either have one or the other. We've all seen what the other half of the population has. Even if one is a virgin," she stopped for a split-second and looked at the wondering faces. "*Is* anyone here a virgin?" Everyone laughed. She quickly continued: "Never mind, you don't have to answer that. As I was saying, you've surely seen the anatomy—in a magazine, a film, statues, or even on a beach." She looked at the giants among men. "Basically, if you don't care I don't care. Just think of me as one of the boys."

"Guys, if you're not comfortable with this we'll figure something else out," Oliver said.

The players looked at each other, grinned and nodded. "Naw, Coach, we're good," one of the players said.

"We don't care, Lady Maxine, no, make that Lord Max since you're one of the boys," Neil said. He looked at his team and winked. The team had welcomed him as their quarterback and leader once they understood that he fought hard to live up to everyone's expectation, including his own. They were a tight knit group and had each other's backs, on the field and off as well. They found that besides being an amazing quarterback Neil really was a good, decent guy and even had a sense of humor. The QB dropped the towel covering his family jewels. His team didn't let him down—they followed suit.

Maxine tried not to laugh at the men playing with her. Instead she smiled nonchalantly and simply said: "Lovely, gentlemen." They didn't miss the double meaning and everyone present laughed. "Thank you for including me in your family," Maxine finished and turned toward Oliver. He was grinning like a Cheshire cat. Boys will be boys and he was one too. As open-minded as she was she didn't want anyone to see the crimson slowly covering her face and neck. She was a girl after all, albeit completely open-minded, but just how often did an entire team of beautiful male bodies affectionately expose themselves? They were playing with her and it was a sort of test. She didn't mind. On the contrary, she understood they had accepted her and were letting her know they were a close-knit family. What she was sure of, however, was the next time she walked into the locker room whatever state of dress or undress the players found themselves in, no one would think anything about it.

CHAPTER 12

BAD GUYS DOWN

Oliver and Maxine left the locker room and headed down the hallway. They met up with William and the three of them walked together. A little farther down Isaac Cohen, the Natives' public relations man, was at his desk devising the best campaign possible for the team. He needed to bring the most publicity to benefit them. He and William had gone over his ideas and the owner had been quite pleased. Of course, William had hired the best money could buy and he was happy as he could already see the splendid results of the publicity man's labor. Isaac was a work horse. He worked all hours of the day and night, and every day of the week, so much so that William told him to slow down. Isaac told his boss he would after the season was over. He had his own way of working and his results were always excellent. And he loved what he did.

Isaac was typing a press release on his laptop when he heard his office door open. At first he didn't turn around as he was trying to finish a sentence. The next thing he knew he was being roughly dragged off his chair and thrown to the floor. A man pinned him down to the floor. Isaac looked up and stared at the ugliest face he had ever seen. It was covered in scars which could only have been made by a knife and the deformed nose had most assuredly been broken several times and never healed properly. Isaac was sure even a mother would be revolted by the sight, but at the moment he was more worried about the ominous knife pointed at his chest.

"Who are you? What do you want?" Isaac whispered, trying to squirm away from the weapon.

"Information," an ominous, raspy voice said. It was a second man Isaac hadn't yet seen and was now hovering ominously above him. "About Neil Howard," he continued.

William, Oliver and Maxine were walking down the hallway passed Isaac's door when they heard a muffled groan. That didn't sound right, Maxine immediately thought, something was very wrong. Her martial arts training and her senses kicked in and were instantly at their sharpest. Her index finger flew to her lips. William and Oliver nodded, they would be quiet. They had heard the moan as well.

The door was slightly ajar and Maxine carefully approached the opening and listened. Silence. And then another groan. She slowly opened it and saw Isaac on the floor, blood oozing from his lips and nose and running down his shirt. She quickly looked around. He was alone. Maxine ran in. William and Oliver followed her. They gently helped Isaac up and sat him in his chair.

"Isaac! What happened?" William asked.

"Two sons-of-bitches jumped me, wanted information," he managed to say through swollen lips. He spit out some blood.

"What kind of information?"

"About Neil. They wanted to know where he was."

Oliver paled, as did William.

"What did you tell them?" Oliver asked.

"I figured they were up to no good. I told them he was probably practicing with the team, but I didn't say where he was. I figured he was probably on his way out."

"Does anyone have any idea where he is?" William asked. He was worried and aggravated, and from what Isaac was saying he was sure the loan sharks were the ones who had beaten him up. He thought that problem had been taken care of and made a mental note to call Uncle Frank. It wasn't easy for William to lose his temper, but this definitely was the time—heads would roll.

"He was in the locker room with the other players," Oliver said.

"We're going to find him and possibly the two guys who attacked you. Will you be okay here?" William asked Isaac.

"I'm coming with you," bloody spittle coming from his mouth as he answered.

"Are you sure?"

"Yes, yes, now let's find Neil. Besides, I'd rather be with you guys and not alone."

They filed out of Isaac's office and headed toward the locker rooms. On the way there Maxine suddenly stopped in front of the men's toilet. "I thought I heard something," she whispered. "I'm going in."

"But that's the men's..."

"Exactly. If they're in there they'll be surprised and think I made a mistake.

"Okay, but if we hear anything or if you call us we'll be right in," Oliver whispered. He didn't like it even though he knew she could handle herself better than any one of them there. But still, it sounded like two heavy hitters from the looks of Isaac's face.

Maxine walked in as if she were going to a ladies' room of any public place. She had, however, been right. The two men who had beaten up Isaac were in front of Neil whose back was pinned against a wall. One of them had the blade just an inch away from his chest.

The other one saw Maxine and turned his back to hide his partner. What was the dumb broad doing in the men's room? "Hey, this is the men's room. Get out of here!" he yelled.

"Oh, I must have made a mistake. Sorry," she giggled girlishly. "Just leaving. I'll leave you boys alone." Maxine had seen what she needed, including Neil and the knife. As she turned to leave, she suddenly whirled around, did a roundhouse kick that connected solidly and painfully with the man's face in front of her, while her other leg came up right after and flew powerfully into the man's crotch. The unexpected and excruciating pain from both areas brought him down to his knees. She jumped on his back and used it to lunge at the one holding the knife. She grabbed his wrist with lightning speed and twisted it so fast and so forcefully that he dropped the blade and his body turned in the opposite direction. It was as Maxine anticipated and she used the man's body as leverage against her own back to throw him against one of the stalls. His head hit the door hard and he crumpled down on the floor out cold. It had taken her less than five seconds to put both of them out of commission.

William, Oliver and Isaac had entered the bathroom just in time for the show. Oliver smiled. William laughed, his anger subsiding and Isaac just stood there, his agony momentarily disappearing as he witnessed Maxine's prowess. When he finally found his voice he asked hoarsely: "Who are you? Steven Segal?"

"Same fighting style, totally different bodies," she chuckled.

The three men clapped.

"Neil, you okay?" Oliver asked.

"Never better, Coach. You got here just in time though, especially Lady Max. Thank you. I will never, ever forget that. That was absolutely amazing!"

"My pleasure, Neil."

"I'll go get security, and I'll make sure this never happens again!" William said, still perturbed. How had they gotten past security? "Oliver and Max, why don't you wait here with these assholes?"

"Sure, we can do that," Maxine said and Oliver nodded.

"Isaac, come with me. Let's get you fixed up."

"Uh, can I use any of this? That was totally brilliant!" The PR man said, always thinking about new ways to promote the team.

"No!" They all said at the same time.

"Pity, that was very unique." Isaac sighed and followed William.

CHAPTER 13

FIRST GAME OF THE SEASON

Albuquerque had outdone itself. The stadium was finished and the city was ready to host the first game of the New Mexico Natives. What would usually have taken a year or two was accomplished in less than six months. It seemed every construction worker in the state, and others who came from as far as Arizona, Colorado, Texas and even Oklahoma had managed to finish the addition in record time for the first game. Maybe it was the excitement of New Mexico having its own team, or perhaps the added incentive of bonuses if they finished in a six-month period. Possibly both. In any event, finished it was, and the stadium looked spectacular. The addition blended in with the rest of the original construction and paint, of course, went a long way to freshen up the venue.

The stadium was full. Every seat was occupied. The spectators were buzzing with excitement as they waited for the first game of the season to start. They now had an NFL home team and the game was the hottest ticket in town and in the football world. The day would be historic as this would be the first ever game of the Natives. The majority of New Mexicans were aficionados of the Broncos, the team 'closest' to home. Others were fans of the Cowboys and quite a few favored the Steelers. But times were changing and now they were proud to be supporters and loyal to the New Mexico Natives, even though they hadn't even seen a game or knew the players very well. The news and sports stations had gotten just enough information to whet everyone's appetite and now the eyes of the nation were on this new team. The New Mexican fans were from Albuquerque, Santa Fe and every corner of the state. They came from Pueblos and Reservations, others stemmed from descendants from exiled Spaniards as well as inhabitants who still lived on the land their ancestors had claimed centuries before. More locals originated from Mexico, Central and South America and migrants from other states who had fallen in love with the Land of Enchantment and now called it home.

The governor of New Mexico, the mayor, the NFL commissioner, the President of the University and members of their families were in the main VIP boxes. Celebrities had been invited who were either originally born in New Mexico, lived in the state part of the year or just had a special place in their heart such as Demi Moore, Ali MacGraw, Neil Patrick Harris, Anna Gunn, Demi Lovato, Julia Roberts, A Martinez, Val Kilmer, Anne Hillerman, Jeff Bezos, the Unser family, Randy Travis, Gene Hackman, Shirley MacLaine, George R. R. Martin, Bryan Cranston, Mai Shanley who was Miss New Mexico and Miss USA, the Native American musician and flute player Robert Mirabal and of course athletes with ties to the state. William had his designer create the most extravagant luxury suites with a glass roof for a 360 degree view of the surrounding mountains and the high desert mesa. Leather armchairs and sofas were placed strategically for perfect observation of the stadium, the surrounding views and the wall-size televisions. A bar and buffet were set up for the guests so they could help themselves to drinks and food, or they could order a favorite dish from each suite's personal chef. All the rooms were filled with celebrity guests who had accepted the invitation.

The broadcasters' booth hosted Tony Schuster, a man in his fifties and longtime commentator, as well as Laura Sullivan, a young woman who was the daughter of a Hall of Famer. It seemed the football great had taught his little girl everything possible about the game. She had grown up in her daddy's shadow and loved football so much that she became an expert. It was said that there wasn't anything she didn't know about America's favorite pastime, including rules and statistics on players, past and present. She also loved what she did—announcing at games and analyzing every aspect of the plays. The two broadcasters had worked together for the past couple of years. They respected each other as colleagues and were always amazed at the other's knowledge. They were also fun and their humor played well to their audience. Tony watched over her like a protective uncle, not that she needed it, but he was old school and a gentleman. He really did care for her as if she were part of his family. The feeling was mutual. Laura loved him like an uncle and he reminded her of her dad. They were of the same generation and ever since her father died she cherished Tony even more. They had that endearing camaraderie of an uncle and niece and shared a love for football. They were a knowledgeable, hearteningly unique duo, and their audience was always pleased when they were the announcers at the game.

"Welcome everyone and thanks for joining us. I'm Tony Schuster and next to me is my amazing colleague Laura Sullivan. We will be with you throughout the game. Today should be interesting…"

"And historic," Laura added.

"Absolutely. It's the first game of the season and the first time this new team, the New Mexico Natives, is making an appearance. Unlike other games where the teams have been around for decades and we've followed them for years and know every statistic about them, well, we don't know much about the Natives yet. Kind of interesting really. I'm actually feeling a little unprepared. How about you Laura?"

"I know what you mean, Tony. We do know the coach, Oliver Hadley, from the New England Patriots. He was always a great assistant coach, but let's see what he's been able to do with his own team."

"From what I understand all these players were guys that didn't make the cut on any of the other NFL teams and wound up here. They probably sleep and dream football and want to prove to the world they belong on the field. That means they're young and hungry."

"But also inexperienced," Laura added.

"You're right. We do know something about Neil Howard. But they must be a little crazy to trust the guy. Nobody in their right mind would put him on their team. He's just not reliable," Tony insisted.

"Yes, we know his background and his problem—who doesn't? But it's the beginning of the season. Let's see what happens. Oliver Hadley has given him a chance to play and I like believing in second chances. Hopefully it will prove positive. Howard was such a brilliant quarterback. He had the quick mind of some of the greats and an arm that could do anything. It would be wonderful if he were back. He was always a joy to watch."

"I know you like him and I hope you're right."

"Hadley used to be part of the Belichick team and many of the great coach's assistants have gone on to triumphant careers. Will Oliver Hadley be included in that elite club? It will be really interesting to see what he's done with the Natives," Laura said.

"I'm thinking this game might just be a flop—brand new in the NFL, players that didn't make any other team and who are now just starting—like pee wee football."

"You're such a pessimist, Tony," Laura said, chuckling. "We know they've worked hard and their team could be promising. You've been around for quite a few years and you know anything could happen on the field."

"Exactly. I have been around, and from all those years of experience I can almost guarantee not only a washout but an unprecedented thrashing."

"Ah, think positively. It is football, after all."

William, Oliver, staff members and players were in the locker room. The head coach observed his young team. They looked sharp in their new tan and dark amber uniforms and were ready to take the field. He gathered them in front of him. They waited. The other coaches and staff were behind Oliver. They too were ready. "Gentlemen, today we are making history. We are the newest football team in the NFL and playing our first game ever."

The players hollered and clapped.

"However," Oliver continued, "many will think that we shouldn't be here, but they would be very wrong. You are great athletes with amazing talent. You *are* bona fide football players and you have worked very hard. I firmly believe we will give them something to talk about. They may think you are rookies and that this is, for most of you, your first professional game. But make no mistake, in addition to your prowess they will also see your great hearts and your love for the game, and you will prove that on the field. I believe, no, I'm sure we can win today. We have studied our opponents and we have some incredible plays that will probably blow their minds."

The players laughed. One of them hollered: "No doubt we're beating them today, Coach!"

"Yeah, we can't lose our very first game," another shouted.

"That's what I like to hear. I believe in you, gentlemen, so let's prove it to the world!"

"Yes, Coach!"

"Would anyone like to say something before we go out?"

"I would, coach," Neil said. "Thank you and Mr. Quinn for this opportunity. I'm pretty sure I speak for all of us when I say that we are grateful. We won't let you down." He turned toward the players. "Right, guys?"

"Right!" They shouted back.

"Thank you," Oliver said. "I'm very proud of each and every one of you." He looked around the room. "Anyone else?"

William said just a few words and let them know how proud he was of how far they had all come and wished them the best. He didn't want to distract them.

"I have something to add," Maxine said.

Everyone in the room focused on her. She had earned their respect and they were attentive. "I just wanted say that you all look very spiffy and quite dashing. You are going to break some hearts out there today, especially when you win, gentlemen."

The men hollered and clapped. They were eager, happy and ready to make their debut. The players and staff left the locker room and headed toward the field.

The weather was perfect with no wind at all. The sun was slowly descending and the fading light hit the Sandia Mountains just right and turned them red.

On each end of the field, at the twenty yard lines and between the markers two hot air balloons baskets were resting on their sides with their envelopes laid out on the grass, their tops toward the end zones. Albuquerque was the capital of the ballooning world and true to form the opening would of course have hot air balloons. The pilots and their crews started inflating the enormous envelopes at the same time. The excitement in the stadium was palpable.

Women, and some men, wore earrings with feather designs. Others sported foam headdresses with painted feathers in the team's colors. Still others drew lines in the colors of the team across their cheeks. In one section of the stadium a group dressed in full Indian regalia, a combination of members of the UNM band and local Native American chanters, were ready to play. Several cellos from the band began the almost hypnotic, yet exquisite sounds of *Yeha Noah*, Wishes of Happiness and Prosperity, by the group Sacred Spirit. The drums gently entered and followed the cellos and the melody. The music put the spectators in a happy mood and the drumming added additional energy to the already enthusiastic crowd.

When the envelopes were almost ready, the crews tipped the baskets up and the pilots stood in their respective gondolas. When they were fully inflated their designs were of the U.S. flag and the other the New Mexico flag with the Zia symbol. The pilots and crews kept the hot air balloons upright but did not take off.

With the sun almost gone the sky transitioned from a magnificent and unique New Mexico sunset of yellows, oranges and violets into a vast blue-black canvas. The fires from the burners made the enormous globes glow every time the pilots needed to keep the hot air balloons upright. The crowd loved it.

The governor, mayor, NFL commissioner and William were on a small stage in the middle of the field. They gave short speeches and waved to the crowd and cameras before leaving to go to their boxes and families. William went to the owner's box where Dezba, Uncle Frank, Roberta and Charles were waiting.

The music and drumming continued and fireworks from around the top of the stadium shot up into the air in a bright display of iridescent colors. The opposing team came running out and went to their side of the grounds.

On the field hot air balloon baskets with just burners but no envelopes were lined up on either side of the fifty yard line up to the first markers. As the Natives' cheerleaders ran out shaking their pompoms the pilots in the gondolas below the burners fired them up and the beautiful young women ran between the rows of fire. When they were at the second set of markers they stopped, posed with one arm in the air and the other by their side. Then they went down the length of the markers and put on a quick show. They continuously shook their pompoms, adding to the already rising enthusiasm of the crowd. Some of the fans came just to watch the lovely ladies and not so much for the game.

It was time for the NFL's newest players to come out and make their debut, but first a dozen runners raised their respective flags and ran through the path between the fires to their designated positions on the field. The flags were sets of three; the U.S. flag, the New Mexico flag, and the team flag proudly showing off its tough Natives logo. The next one to come out was the team mascot, the native man from one of the Pueblos. He wore a leather vest dyed ombré, the colors ranging from tan to burnt orange from the neck to the waist and with the team logo on the front and back. The pants were also leather and the same burnt orange. The ensemble looked like the team's uniforms and mimicked the colors of the New Mexico desert and skies. He also wore a magnificent headdress of feathers, the majority the colors of the team. Necklaces, bracelets, all decorated with turquoise and silver, two elements of the once state's economic wealth, adorned the mascot's neck, wrists and ankles. The jewelry, clothing and feathers which he wore had been blessed and offered by the tribes of the nineteen Pueblos and three Reservations of New Mexico. He also carried a wand covered with feathers and a football crowned the top. He ran to the center of the field through the path of fire from the hot air balloon burners and stopped on the Natives logo prominently displayed on the grass. Then, for the very first time in their history, it was time for the players of the New Mexico Natives to take their field. They followed the mascot, led by Neil Howard, their quarterback and each player ran behind him and through the alley of fire. As they did their faces were portrayed on the jumbotron. The fans did their part and welcomed them with shouts and clapping. The players stopped in a circle around the mascot. When they were all present they took a knee. The music, which had been playing the entire time, faded out. Suddenly the mascot raised the wand, held it high over his head and yelled out: "HONEEZNÁ! WIN!" Then he did a few dance steps reminiscent of Indian Pow Wows and the players got up and mirrored the same steps. It was a ritual they would come to do at the beginning of each game. The crowd went crazy and whooped out cries and did the steps in the stands as well.

William, who was now in the owner's box shouted: "Come on everybody!" as he saw the players in the middle of the field. He started dancing as well. Dezba joined him enthusiastically. The VIPs, celebrities and their entourage followed suit. Roberta and Charles, always good sports and never shy, joined in too.

A cameraman for one of the television channels capturing the dancing realized it was not only on the field and in the stands, but in the VIP boxes as well. He swung his camera around and suddenly they too were projected on the jumbotron stadium screen and on televisions around the country. The spectators immediately cheered, chanted and danced along with them.

"Now there's a scene you don't see every day," Tony said.

"That is so cool!" Laura said as she got up from her stool and did her own mini dance. The footage of the announcer and the celebrities would go viral. Isaac Cohen couldn't be happier.

The cameraman panned back to the field. The mascot once again raised his wand and shouted: "HONEEZNÁ! WIN!" The players repeated it, and the fans all around the stadium did as well as the drummers beat rhythms on the drums.

The cheerleaders and the players left the field and went to the sidelines. The military came out and instead of holding an enormous American flag they marched to the hot air balloons and made a circle around them. An announcer asked the spectators to please rise for the anthem. One of the local beloved celebrity singers had gotten into the U.S. balloon. As soon as the baskets slowly rose up, the U.S. one first and the Zia one slightly lower, the singer began the national anthem. New Mexico was proud of its service and military tradition and it was reflected in the scene playing out before their eyes. The hot air balloons hovered in place just above the military representatives. When the anthem ended the pilots descended back to the grass and the singer climbed out with the help of a pair of gallant Marines who effortlessly lifted her out. The flyers once again fired up the burners and this time they rose up and above the stadium. The spectators watched the fires lift them away from the venue. They could be seen for several miles as they ascended higher and seemed to float among the burgeoning stars. They would eventually land and their chase crews would pick them up.

The servicemen and women marched off the field, the opening concluded. It was time for the game.

"Wow! That's probably the most amazing and unique intro I've ever seen!" Laura said enthusiastically.

"I'll second that. That really was spectacular, from the music to the cheerleaders to the military and those beautiful hot air balloons portraying the American and New Mexico flags."

"And amazing pilots and crews. I'm sure it's pretty difficult to keep the balloons from rising like that."

"Well, this is it, Laura, time for the very first game of the New Mexico Natives."

"I'm really excited but it's quite different when you haven't seen any of the players. We know their positions and that's about it. The only ones we really know anything about is Oliver Hadley and Neil Howard. Oh, this is going to be fun, Tony."

"Now who is that on the Natives side over there? That woman, is she the cheerleaders' coach or something?"

"No, she's an assistant coach and she's a Brit. Lady Maxine Owen-Smith to be exact."

"What? Does she know anything about football?" Tony asked incredulously.

"Well, she's a Royal from across the pond."

"She's English and a member of the Queen's family?"

"That's right, Tony. From what I hear everybody's really impressed with her. She's a professor at Oxford, an expert in military strategies. Apparently her mind works like a chess master. She helps the Coach develop plays."

"Seriously?"

"Uh, huh."

"What is this game coming to?" Tony groaned.

"I hear she's amazing, and she's not bad to look at."

"That's true. She really is a beautiful woman. Brains and beauty, it does sound like a winning combination."

"Sure does. I hope she and the coach are an item," Laura grinned.

"Oh, you're a romantic too?"

"Hey, I have my moments," she chuckled.

"Hadley doesn't miss a trick."

Tony became very interested. He had witnessed just about everything about the sport, but a military strategist? Really? *And* she was English and a woman? This was a first for him and the butterflies in his stomach confirmed his excitement.

The opposition received the ball first. They were an old established team. The coaches and players had been together for years and were cocky with their experience. They would be careful but assumed they would simply thrash the rookies as if they were players fresh out of high school. They certainly didn't expect, however, the level of readiness that came at them. The Natives defensive line held them back as well as any team on the circuit. They didn't score a touchdown on their first drive and the kicker missed the field goal. Their overconfidence hadn't kept them sharp enough. The score remained empty, and the Natives fans were ecstatic—it was going better than they could have anticipated and they were thrilled. They even helped out by shouting as loud as they could during the opposing team's plays.

Music had the power to push people up in the best of ways. The drumming and tunes from the stands boosted everyone's energy and enthusiasm, fans and players alike. The Natives' offensive line took the field for the first time in their history. They looked sharp in their new uniforms and pride exuded from every player running into position.

One of the plays the Natives practiced continuously, and had become one of Oliver's favorites, was the Oxford. They named it in Maxine's honor and they were going to try it.

Neil called out: "Ten, twenty-three, Oxford, Oxford..."

The opposing defensive players looked at him. What the hell was Oxford? They would soon find out.

"Hut, hut." The center snapped the ball to Neil who faked a handoff to the running back, but Neil turned slightly and faked another handoff to the fullback. The defense lunged at the quarterback thinking Neil still had the ball but Neil turned again slightly and faked another pass. The opponents finally noticed that the first handoff to the running back was real and the man was running down the field until one of the safeties finally stopped him.

"What was that?" Tony bellowed, "a triple fake?"

"*And* thirty yards!" Laura exclaimed. "That was beautifully done."

"I'll say."

The opposing team was now much more attentive. They hadn't expected The Natives to execute their first play so well.

The players were in position waiting for the Natives' quarterback. Neil obliged them: "Ten, twenty-three, New York, New York!"

What was it with city names the opposition wondered?

The ball was snapped into Neil's hands and the offensive players on the line of scrimmage shifted one step to the left. When Oliver had seen this the first time during practice he couldn't help but think of a chorus line and called the play New York. The players liked the city names. It made it easier to remember the plays. Neil tossed the ball to the right where his tight end caught it just next to him and took off fast toward the end zone, side stepping a lineman. He was stopped on the ten-yard line.

"Well, that didn't take long, they're just ten yards away from a touchdown," Tony said.

"That's right, it'll be their first."

"Let's see if they can do it."

"I bet you they make it, Tony."

Both teams were at the line of scrimmage waiting when suddenly one of the Natives players stepped across before he was supposed to. The false start cost them five yards. They lined up again, this time on the fifteen.

Neil received the snap, took a couple of steps back and aimed at one of his receivers. Unfortunately he was too heavily covered, as was every other player, so he took off.

"Howard's running! He's on the ten, the five..." Tony rattled on almost as fast as Neil was running.

Four defensemen surrounded Neil. They were just

inches away from him. No way were they going to let the QB through and Neil knew it. He stopped as abruptly as he could the moment the opponents lunged at him which gave him the split-second he needed. As they went down towards his waist and legs Neil jumped up high, lifted his knees to his chest and threw himself above them and managed to roll over a couple of the players' backs and flopped into the end zone for a touchdown.

"He made it through! It's the Natives' first touchdown ever!" Lauren screamed.

"Unbelievable! What a play!"

The fans in the stands went crazy screaming and hollering.

The mascot at the back shouted: "HONEEZNÁ!" The team ran to the end zone, lifted Neil up and smacked him everywhere from his helmet to his backside. They all quickly lined up in a circle, did a couple of the steps they had done during the introduction before the beginning of the game with the mascot and shouted "HONEEZNÁ!"

"That's probably the best touchdown celebration I've ever seen and I bow down to you, young lady. You were right. This is football and the outcome is never guaranteed."

The fans mimicked the steps as the Natives' music and drumming resonated throughout the stadium.

Oliver watched the replay on the enormous screen and smiled from ear to ear when Maxine became as big the jumbotron as she energetically moved to the Natives' music and did the celebratory steps as well. 'That's my girl, she is magnificent,' Oliver thought to himself. He could have watched a replay on the screen all day.

By the end of the fourth quarter both teams were tied with three touchdowns each. Oliver didn't want to go into overtime. His players had been great but he could tell they were exhausted and their lack of experience would now hinder them if they had to go into extra time. They had the ball and they had to score. There were only ten seconds left on the clock when Oliver spoke into the microphone. Neil listened carefully to his coach's words and relayed the instructions to his team in the huddle.

On the line of scrimmage the players were ready for another of Maxine's strategic plays.

"If he scores the Natives will win the game!" Laura exclaimed.

"Yes, the clock is almost out of time!" Tony added.

"Ten, twenty-three, Tokyo! Tokyo!" Neil hollered. The ball was snapped into his hand, he did a stutter step, faked a pass to the running back, lifted himself off the ground about a foot as his arm went up to pass the ball to the tight end who was running into the end zone. Neil was a combination matador and ballet dancer but didn't release the ball. The opposing defensemen, one who was jumping up to stop the ball, and the other who was ready to lunge at Neil were momentarily stunned as they watched the QB do a move they had never seen before. It seemed unnatural. It was part of the *ukemi* from the Aikido exercise that Maxine had shown the Natives in practice. Neil seemed to be falling and his back, almost parallel to the ground so the linebackers thought he would be down in an instant. Instead, Neil lifted himself back up and ran past the stunned defensemen and into the end zone for the game's final touchdown.

The crowd went wild. They screamed and shouted for joy as did the rest of the team and staff. They hugged and congratulated each other and the mascot and the players did their winning dance.

"That was an amazing play by Neil Howard! He's

looking better than he ever has!" Tony said.

"Indeed he does and he led his team all the way. If he keeps it up the season looks bright for him and the Natives."

"What a game! And congratulations to the newest team in the league. Hadley and the owner William Quinn must be very proud of them!"

"I'll say! We know so much more about the players, these rookies who everyone was ready to wash the floor with have shown the world that they are to be reckoned with. I'm sure all of us who watched today can hardly wait for their next game. What a terrific job. They played hard and with heart," Laura said.

"Yes, I agree. And although they did make some mistakes, which was to be expected being they're first-timers and a new team, they were terrific and inspiring. Ladies and gentlemen, we thank you for spending this historic day with us and we will connect with you again very soon. I'm Tony Schuster, along with Laura Sullivan. Until next time we bid you goodbye."

After the game, once the players were all in the locker room, William hugged and thanked each one of them. Everyone present was jumping up and down, hollering at the top of their lungs. It was their first game *and* their first win. They truly believed they were on top of the world and would hopefully always stay there.

"How do we feel?" Oliver shouted to his players.

"HONEEZNÁ!" They shouted back the Navajo word.

"And what did the other team do?" Oliver demanded to know.

"BAA HONEEZNÁ! They lost!"

They whooped around, hugged each other and

laughed. A couple of them even shed a tear. Today the Natives made history—it was the first game of a new team. They were the first players and they had won. No one present, or anyone affiliated with the team or the fans would ever forget this day.

Neil Howard raised his arms and quieted everyone down. They did and watched as he walked up to William and presented a ball to him. It was signed by all the players, the coaches and the staff, down to the water boy. The quarterback asked him to sign it. "This is the ball that scored the first New Mexico Natives touchdown. We've all signed it. You're the only one who hasn't."

"You want me to sign this?"

"Yes, Sir, once you put your John Hancock on it, it will be complete—the entire and first New Mexico Natives team. We'd like you to maybe put it in trophy case so that everyone will be able to see it," Neil said. He handed a marker to the owner.

William immediately signed and then looked up at the faces watching him. The man could not have been any prouder. "This is truly an honor, as it is to be among you, you who are an amazing group of people and what I am sure will be one of the best teams ever! Thank you all very much. I will display this with great pride for everyone to admire!"

They hollered and jumped up and down, hugged and smacked each other. It was a beginning, one they had started, and a day no one would ever forget.

CHAPTER 14  THE SWEAT

After the game Neil Howard drove his rental car through Albuquerque. He took in the bright stars above the mesa of the high desert and marveled at how far he could see the lights of the city and the surrounding areas. He hadn't felt this good in a very long time and his mind meticulously analyzed why. Most importantly his parents were safe and he was debt free and rid of loan sharks. William had put an end to any further problems with his debts and the goons who retaliated. He had heard that the owner had given someone hell and it hadn't been pretty. He was just grateful that no one was after him anymore. He was playing football with a bunch of really good guys and coached by an amazing staff. They played their first game as a new team and won! He was their quarterback and he proved he could be a good leader. He respected his guys and pumped them up. He showed them how much he loved the game and how much they meant to him. They in turn tried their best to live up and reciprocate his standards. Neil mused that at twenty-four he was the oldest and most seasoned player on the Natives team. This really was a young team and boy did they have heart. How much sweeter could that be?

He wanted to celebrate and unwind, and his subconscious drove him in the direction he had always gone after a game, whether the team had won or not. The city was easy to get around in and Neil found himself in front of a twenty-four hour establishment—it was always open—the Sandia casino on the outskirts of town. He could see it was well maintained, pristine and inviting. Neil loved everything about it, from the architecture to the parking lots. And that's where he stopped. He was excited. He hadn't gambled in quite a while and his stomach was churning in blissful anticipation. The first thing he would do was smell. There was a distinct aroma to gambling. Maybe it was the plastic of the chips, the felt on the tables or the steel of the slot machines.

But something, maybe a voice in his head, held him back for a moment. Before leaving the car Neil took a deep breath and suddenly the image of Oliver Hadley appeared in his windshield. Oh, right, he had promised his coach *and* himself he would live up to his end of the deal, mainly no gambling whatsoever. How would the coach find out, anyway? Easy, he would just find a high roller room with the well-known privacy. *Idiot*, he chastised himself, *you just became one of the most recognized faces in New Mexico.*

Neil dismissed the logic and Oliver put his hand on the door to open it, but he noticed his hands trembling. His hands couldn't shake! He was a quarterback! He needed his body to be pristine, one hundred percent ready for the next workout, the next game. He closed his eyes, trying to block everything out, but gaming chips were dancing and spinning in front of his mind's eye.

I shouldn't. I'm not supposed to, Neil said to himself, but he was being torn by the two voices in his head. *I have to. It's stronger than I am. No, I'm stronger, I don't want to ruin my life.* Neil opened his eyes and started screaming and hitting the steering wheel—rage, frustration and addiction enveloping him. Finally he began to cry. With trembling hands he picked up his cell phone and looked at the numbers. They were blurry from the tears but thankfully the coach's number was the first one on his list. Had he anticipated this and put Hadley's number before even the emergency 911 number? His shaky fingers made the call.

"Hello?" Oliver answered. There was no sound from the other end. "Hello?" He repeated.

"Coach?" It was barely a whisper.

Oliver thought he recognized the voice. "Neil, is that you?"

"Yeah, Coach."

"Are you alright? Where are you?"

"In the car."

"Were you in an accident?" It was the first thing Oliver could think of as the man's voice sounded as if he were in physical pain.

"No."

Silence.

"Neil, tell me where you are." Oliver asked again. Now he was getting really worried.

"Coach," he said crying, "I'm in a car I rented… parked in front of the Sandia casino."

Oliver closed his eyes and cursed inwardly. He could hear the staccato breaths from the crying. "Neil…"

"Coach, you said to call you if I had a problem," Neil sobbed.

"I did, and I'm glad you called me. I'm leaving right now. I'll be there in less than fifteen minutes. Promise me you won't move and you'll wait in the car."

"Coach…" Neil couldn't continue.

Oliver snatched the keys off the kitchen counter and ran out. "Neil! Promise me!" He hollered.

"I'll be right here, Coach. I'm in a silver car in the lot

in front of the main entrance," Neil said and hung up.

"Neil! Neil!"

Oliver tried calling back, but the man wasn't picking up. He dialed Dezba.

"Yes?" She answered.

"Sorry, Dezba, I know it's late, but we've got a problem. I want to run something by you. Let me know if you know anything about it and if you can help me with this."

"What's wrong?" She asked, instantly alert. Oliver would never call unless something was very wrong.

"It's Neal. You of course know about his problem."

"I do."

"I'm on my way to the casino. He hasn't gone in and kudos to him for calling me. That probably was one of the hardest things he ever had to do."

"I agree, but what is it I can help with?"

"Sweat lodge," he said simply.

"A sweat lodge? To do what? For Neil?"

"Yes, I know it's probably a long shot but I think it could help. Right?" Oliver was desperate. "I've been following some buddies, vets that came back from Iraq and Afghanistan. They swear by it, especially to help with PTSD. They found the results were better than conventional medicine. I've also heard it helps kick an alcohol or a drug habit, maybe it could help with his gambling problem."

"I think it's definitely worth a try."

"Yeah? Great! Do you know how we go about this?"

"I do. I've got a sweat lodge close to my place on the Rez."

"Really?"

"Uh, huh. Listen, get to Neil and keep him there. I'll call my brother, Ahiga, and we'll meet up, then he'll take him under his proverbial wing. He'll take care of the sweat."

"Dezba, you are a godsend! And so is Ahiga! Thank you both so much."

Oliver found Neil and immediately made him get into his car. The man was shaking as if going through a narcotic withdrawal.

"It's going to be alright, Neil."

"How Coach? Why can't I stop?" He asked, praying that he would be given an answer. Neil looked as if all the blood had drained from his face. He was deathly pale.

"I want you to trust me. I have an idea that might help."

Neil nodded. "I trust you more than anyone in the world. I'm sorry, Coach, I know it's late…"

"No, I'm glad you did. Besides, I'm the one who insisted you call me, remember?"

Neil nodded again. "How do I get over this?" He whimpered.

"It's an addiction, like drugs or alcohol. I have an idea that might help. Please try it and go along with it."

"I have faith in you, Coach, and I'll try anything at this point."

"Thanks, Neil, I believe in you too. You're too special to let this ruin your life."

"I know," he whimpered. "I've been there. I ruined my career and I put my parents through living hell, not to mention how many fans I let down. I don't want to do that anymore. I just want to be the best quarterback I can be, give my parents a life they deserve and at some point maybe have a nice little family. I'm not asking for the moon, am I?"

"Couple kids, a dog and a cat?" Oliver asked, trying to lighten the mood.

Neil smiled. "Yeah, that would be nice."

"Okay, let's aim for that dream. Now, I just ask you to trust me."

"Of course, Coach, anything you say. Uh, am I still on the team?"

"You are, but first I need you to try something before any games or even practice. Once you've done this you're back and we'll take it from there."

Oliver looked at the young man. He had such a bright future in front of him. He would try anything to make sure he could follow that path. Kicking him off the team didn't do anyone any good, not Neil, the players or even himself. He was a good quarterback and a good guy. The players looked up to him and believed in him. Oliver believed in second chances. By calling him Neil had shown some restraint and hadn't gone blindly into the casino. That was a hell of a good sign.

"What did you have in mind?" Neil asked.

"Dezba and Ahiga, her brother, are on their way. They should be here any minute. Agiha is going to take you to the Reservation where they're from and you're going to spend a day or two there."

Neil had absolutely no idea what Oliver had in store for him. "What are we going to do there?"

"You'll see when you get there. Ahiga will give you more details on the way." Oliver looked at his quarterback. "I'm going to do everything I can for you, Neil. I need to know you'll give me your best try, just like on the field, and you won't let me down."

"I will try my best, Coach. I want this just as much as you do, even more actually. Does anyone know…"

"No, just Dezba and Ahiga. I of course had to tell

William and Maxine, but they're cool."

"Yes, they are, and so are you, Coach. I don't know how to thank you."

"Yes, you do. There's only one way, and that's to kick this shit out of your system and be the best man you can be, on the field and in life."

A pickup that had seen better days drove up next to them and stopped. Dezba and Ahiga got out. Oliver and Neil did the same.

"Thank you both very much," Oliver said to the brother and sister.

Standing next to the petite woman was a giant. They looked up at the seven foot colossal Native American man. He was probably one of the biggest men Oliver and Neil had ever seen. He sported a mane of black hair neatly tied back in a ponytail and a very square jaw that truly looked unbreakable.

"This is Ahiga, my little brother."

"Nice to meet you," Oliver said and wondered what happened to the two feet that differentiated the siblings. Under different circumstances Oliver would have liked to talk to Ahiga, but this wasn't the time.

They all embraced, more like a family than anything else, almost as if two members were going off to war. Ahiga and Dezba knew that Neil had a fight on his hands and that he needed to confront it. Oliver left in his car, Dezba drove Neil's back.

Ahiga headed out toward the Reservation and explained some things about a sweat lodge. They drove in silence. Every once in a while when Ahiga felt his energy draining or just needed time to think, he would go for a sweat. It helped him through the dark and difficult times. He would drift into a place of blankness and peace, where his mind would float soothingly in a tranquil space. Neil, on the other hand, wasn't sure what to expect, but he would do everything Ahiga would tell him. He desperately wanted to be free of this affliction. He didn't think the sweat lodge would be a cure, but every little bit could help and he would try his best.

They arrived in less than an hour and Ahiga drove straight to the sweat lodge near his home. It was far enough from other little houses or trailers and desolate enough as to not be bothered by any neighbors. It was still the middle of the night and most everyone was asleep. The two men hadn't said more than a few words, but Neil had thanked Ahiga profusely on their drive. The big man nodded but kept thinking that this wouldn't be a picnic for the brilliant quarterback.

They parked the car and walked a few yards to their destination. Ahiga picked up some wood and kindling and started a fire near the sweat lodge. He quickly went into his house and came out with a sack of supplies.

The skeleton of the hut, which Ahiga built in a round formation, was made of small juniper trees, branches and boughs. The structure was sealed with mud and cedar bark and there was an opening in the top for the smoke. There was a large hole right below in the center of the lodge that would hold the embers and hot stones. He also left an opening to go in and out, framed it with wood and built a door. Although it was a bit of a modern touch he figured it was easier than throwing a blanket over the opening and the purpose was the same.

Neil watched as Ahiga built a fire and put fairly large stones around it.

"Neil, you need to take your clothes off," Ahiga said.

"All of them?"

"As far as you want, underwear is fine. All is fine too."

Neil nodded and stripped to his skivvies. Ahiga laughed when he saw they were Ellen DeGeneres underwear.

"What? They're comfortable," Neil insisted.

Ahiga stripped down to his underpants as well. The night was cold but the fire kept them warm.

"It's time. Let's start. The sweat lodge helps you through dark and difficult times. It also helps kick addictions. You may not think much about it, but keep an open mind and go with the flow," Ahiga said.

Neil wasn't sure what the flow was and he thought a sweat lodge wouldn't do a damn thing for his gambling problem, but he had promised Coach that he would go through with it and he would keep his word. Besides, it would only be for a day or two and he was sure he could endure that. "I will."

Ahiga faced the fire and told Neil to stand across from him on the other side of the flames. When they were in position the big man closed his eyes and raised his arms shoulder height and turned his palms upward.

"Spirits of the North, Spirits of the South, Spirits of the East, Spirits of the West," Ahiga invoked and each time he turned in the direction of the cardinal points. He made an offering of tobacco to the Creator, to the Grandfathers and Grandmothers. Ahiga took Neil's hands and held them above the fire. He prayed for protection, for peace, for healing, for wisdom. He pulled out a shell lined with mother of pearl and some sage from his bag. He lit the crumpled leaves in the vessel and when they were glowing and the men could smell its sweet aroma, Ahiga hovered the shell above Neil's head. With an eagle feather he fanned the smoke all around the man and started chanting. When he finished he asked Neil to sage him as well. The quarterback did, respecting the tradition of his Native American buddy. Ahiga brought out a drum from the bag and started beating a rhythm, singing and dancing around the fire. Neil followed him, without dancing or chanting. He just walked. Between the heat, the incantation and the sage Neil started feeling a little light-headed.

As the fire turned to embers Ahiga transferred the hot coal to the fire pit in the lodge with a shovel. He also took the glowing stones and placed them one by one on top of the embers. The first stone he placed facing West, the next one North, then East and South, and in the center a few more for all people. Neil watched as Ahiga performed the ritual his tribe had done for so many centuries. The lodge became hot and steamy.

"Have a seat," Ahiga said.

They sat on the earth with their bare backs against the body of the hut. Ahiga dipped a cup into a bucket of water, poured it over the hot stones and called forth the Spirit Guides from the four directions. The steam whistled and undulated in the red glow of the lodge. He put some cedar leaves and sage over the embers. It smelled sweet and Ahiga explained that it had medicinal properties. The smoke filled their nostrils, their sinus passages opened and their lungs expanded. The two men started to perspire after only a few minutes. In just a short time Neil was sure that every ounce of liquid was coming out of his body. Ahiga seemed to read the other man's mind.

"When you bathe you are cleaning the outside of your skin. When you do a sweat you are cleansing the inside of your body, both physically and spiritually."

"I understand."

"Sky Father, cleanse our spirit, guide us on our paths, send forth your love and mercy, protect us from evil and unwanted addictions," Ahiga prayed.

The big man recited the first verse of the Navajo sweat lodge song. Throughout the night they would go in and out of the hut several times.

They covered their wet bodies with sand and let it dry with the air. Before going back in they would rub it off. At some point during the night Neil came out coughing and firmly believed the tears from his eyes were gushing the very last of the liquid left in his body. His lungs and body were releasing the toxins and negativity.

"A sweat lodge is like the womb of a mother," Ahiga explained when he came back in. "It is dark and hot, and when you come out you cough and cry. What we are recreating is a rebirth, a spiritual rebirth."

"Makes a lot of sense," Neil wheezed.

After each time they reentered, Ahiga would sing another verse. He repeated the ritual until the entire song had been sung.

Neil lost track of time and didn't know how many hours had passed. The last time they were outside was just before dawn. Since then they had stayed in the lodge and Neil drifted in and out.

After hours into the sweat he watched himself through his mind's eye. He was at a casino, sitting at a blackjack table in his football jersey surrounded by players. They were all big men and looked even bigger because they had their shoulder pads on. He looked at their faces and realized they were members of his team. Behind the players were rows of spectators from the stands. Everyone was laughing at him, making fun of him. He was embarrassed. He tried not to look at them. He focused instead on the dealer behind the table. But it wasn't just one dealer it was three—his parents and

Coach Oliver. They each held a deck of cards. The bottom card of each stack faced him. The same word was written on each card: *Loser!* He looked away and played with the chips in his hands and focused on what his next move would be when one of the now faceless dealers gave give him his next card. He went for the card but before touching it the chips suddenly ignited in his hands. Neil couldn't move from the chair and couldn't move any part of his body. He watched helplessly as his right hand and arm burned into nothingness and smoke. He screamed out loud. He was in agony. He couldn't physically feel the pain of the fire, but the vision of his missing limb up to his shoulder was more devastating than any excruciating pain. The fire was his addiction and it burned his career, but most of all it was burning his soul. The hallucinating images did, however, affect him physically as his stomach violently released its contents.

Ahiga smiled as he watched with gratification the detoxing and releasing of Neil's demons.

CHAPTER 15  THE PLANE

William never wasted time. Once he knew what he wanted he put the gears in motion and made things happen. He pushed one of the most used numbers on his cell phone.

"Hello, Will, what's up? Are we going somewhere?" Scott Malcomb, the Citation's pilot answered. They had been together for years, ever since William had purchased the private plane, and Captain Malcomb had come highly recommended. Scott really liked his boss. He wasn't a pompous or arrogant rich guy who thought of nothing but himself, or how he could make even more money, although he was really good at doing that. No, William was a decent guy who was more of a big boy who did like toys but was still down to earth, had a good heart and was good to his employees. He was fair and very gallant with his money and never missed the opportunity to help wherever he could. The man figured he had plenty for several lifetimes and why not help make peoples' lives a little easier and perhaps happier. Scott was one those employees who was lucky enough to have William as a boss and truly appreciated him. Even though he was on call 24/7 and 365 days a year he loved what he did. He flew William at a moment's notice wherever he needed or wanted to go, whether it was a few days' vacation on

Necker Island, or for a meeting in any of the world capitals or celebrity hideaways. Scott wasn't married and didn't have children so he didn't have the responsibilities that came with a family. And he reaped the benefits of seeing the world as only a select few could. Yes, life was good and Scott was grateful.

"I'm not sure yet. Actually it depends on you," William answered.

"Oh?"

"I need some information on a plane. I want to buy one for the team to fly them to games."

"You know you can charter a commercial carrier," Scott said.

"Yes, but it's a pain. We have over one hundred people, including players, coaches and the traveling staff. And I know the big guys really have a hard time with the seats. I firmly believe that if everyone is happy, players and staff alike, the outcome of the game can be better. We wouldn't have to rely on the commercial airlines, and then there's all the equipment which adds up to thousands of pounds. In the long run it actually would be cheaper and if the team no longer exists, something which we will fight to never let happen, we can always sell it to another organization. And when they see how we'll reconfigure the interior to conform to our players, they'll jump on it."

Scott knew what a keen businessman William Quinn was and he was proving it again. "I think it's a brilliant idea," Scott simply said.

William was happy to hear this. "Yeah? Really?"

"Really." And he meant it.

"Great! Let's get started. Now, you're the expert, what kind of plane would you suggest?"

"Well, the Boeing 737 is a little small, so is the 757.

The 747 is a beautiful bird, but it's really big and getting old. Most of the airlines are getting rid of them. When I flew commercially, I liked the 767 the best. It's a sturdy plane, reliable and a good size. That would be my choice."

"That's the one then. Where can we get one?" William asked excitedly.

Scott chuckled. His boss was really like a boy ready to go into a toy store where he could take home anything he wanted. "When do you want to do this?"

"Yesterday?"

William and Scott embarked on the project and had a meeting with Oliver and the other coaches, as well as the heads of the traveling staff. They all told him what they needed down to the last detail. William knew the design team would come through. He wanted everything done fast and efficiently and he didn't mind spending extra to make it happen. William Quinn always got what he wanted. Working for the billionaire was demanding, albeit exciting. His team of employees would make it happen. They, too, were excited.

Scott did his own homework, online, on the phone and with owners of 767's. When he was satisfied with what he believed he and William were looking for they flew off with the Citation X to meet the seller. They were happy with what they saw and found exactly what they wanted. William paid a little over six million dollars for the used 767 and it was ferried to Albuquerque. When it landed at the airport it was taxied directly to its new home, the hangar William had rented to park it and for its renovations.

As soon as the plane entered the hangar William, Dezba, Captain Scott and the design team were waiting.

William knew the head designer from previous projects such as his luxury yacht and the VIP boxes at the stadium. The designers were excited to be working on another Quinn project. William was demanding yet fun to please, and of course, he paid handsomely.

Everyone present was excited with the new project. The hangar workers pushed the rolling stairs up to the aircraft door. They went up the ramp and stepped aboard. They greeted the pilot who had flown the 767 in, and William and Scott gave the design team a quick tour. William already liked the ideas they were coming up with as they looked around the plane. Their next meeting would be in three days. They left the designer and his team and deplaned.

As scheduled William met with the designer and was shown mock-ups of the interior and the exterior. They had outdone themselves. They worked around the clock the first day and had the plans and drawings finished. The second day they refined the details and built the miniature for William to see, understand better and to make necessary changes. They slept most of the third day and that afternoon they showed their client the designs. The chief designer started with the interior. The cabin and the overhead compartments were tan. The carpeting was a dark amber. The seats were designed for the most comfort. They would all be the same size—spacious, large enough to accommodate even the biggest linebackers, with enough room to stretch their legs out completely, especially since most players were taller than six feet. The seats could swivel to face other seats. They would also be able to recline to almost 180° and not completely flat which was the perfect level to sleep as airplanes are not perfectly straight when they fly. The large overhead compartments would have pillows and warm duvet comforters. There would also be USB ports and a large touchscreen which would come out of the armrests for movies and music. The seats would be equal to any commercial first class luxury accommodation with soothing colors of dark amber leather surrounded by decorative tan ridges. It would match the team colors. Behind the flight deck and in the back the already built-in galleys would be completely updated and stocked with food and beverages.

William listened attentively. He was pleased. The team would be comfortable traveling, and the team colors would help boost morale. The designer was one of the best in the world and was the type of guy who knew exactly what his clients wanted before they even did. He and William were comfortable with each other, having worked together before. When he was finished with the explanation he looked at William and waited for his answer.

"Amazing job. I like it."

"That's great, Will," the man said, let me show you the exterior now." He pulled out a drawing of the plane with the design for the outer paint job. Following the team colors the aircraft was painted in tones of tan to dark amber, blending gradually from the nose to the tail making the design resemble a beautiful wavy sunset. On the fuselage the team name, 'New Mexico Natives', was written across its entire length. On the side of each engine, as well as on both sides of the tail, the team logo was prominently displayed.

"It's absolutely beautiful!" William exclaimed, the boyhood energy always present. "What do you think, Dezba?" He asked turning to her.

"She's stunning. She'll be the envy of every team out there."

William grinned. He was happy and liked being unique. "Anybody have any comments or suggestions?" No one answered. They couldn't think of anything the designers hadn't already thought of. The billionaire turned to the designer and simply said: "Go for it!"

CHAPTER 16

The players were waiting for the bus to take them to the airport. They were always prompt. They knew about Oliver's emphasis on punctuality. Neil was among them. As soon as he had finished the sweat with Ahiga Oliver immediately made him practice with the team. He kept him busy most of the day, leaving him little time to relax. At night Neil was so exhausted he only wanted to sleep. The few times he did think about gambling his stomach reacted the same way it had during the sweat—he would get extremely nauseous. Addictions were difficult and Neil knew that he was the only one who could get a handle on it. He wanted to be rid of it and he knew that the only way he would be successful was if he wanted it badly enough and fought for it. He was grateful for Oliver Hadley and for Ahiga. They were amazing guys who were behind him one hundred percent. He would try his best not to let anyone down.

The bus arrived, the players boarded and the driver took them to the airport. They took a private road and drove onto the tarmac. They stopped in front of one of the hangars. The players looked around and at each other. Why were they here? Why weren't they going to a plane that would take them to the game? And why was their coach standing in front of the big hangar door?

Oliver stepped on the bus and motioned for them to get off. "Hi guys, we have a surprise for you. Come on out," he said.

The players did as he asked and stood in front of the bus.

"You know how much the owner, William Quinn, loves the team," Oliver stated.

They nodded. They actually knew that.

"Well, he went above and beyond, uh, all puns intended. Take a look at what he did," Oliver chuckled and banged on the hanger door. It slowly opened and the players started seeing the New Mexico Natives plane in all its freshly renovated and painted glory. It of course looked like new.

"I expect you will treat your ride with respect."

The main group was present: William, Dezba, Oliver, Maxine, George and Isaac. The players checked out their private plane with awe, respect and excitement. They scrambled aboard and marveled at the luxurious cabin where they would travel to their away games. They all still wondered how lucky they were to be on a professional football team and part of a caring organization.

The group taxied out to the runway and took off toward their destination. They were going to enjoy getting there.

The flight back to Albuquerque was not as pleasant. They had lost the game. The players were grumpy and disappointed. Maybe they were a little overconfident from their first game. The players expected a verbal thrashing from Oliver after their loss, but he surprised them.

Oliver stood at the front of the cabin and looked at his players. "Gentlemen, it's our first loss, and it happens to the best of teams," he said. "There are many things we can do better and we will. We have a lot of work to do and I have no doubt the Natives will go far." The players and staff looked at him. A loss was a loss and it was their first. It was bitter. Oliver continued without yelling or any kind of lashing, just guidance. "I know we weren't our best tonight. It happens. It was our first away game. Our next one is at home, in our stadium, with our fans, and with a lot more practice under our belts. Now that you have tasted the bitterness our next win will be so much sweeter."

Maxine thought she could lighten the mood a little. "Guys, you've probably heard the old adage 'you've lost the battle but you haven't lost the war'. So chins up. Our goal is to make it to the end. Right?!"

"Right!" The players answered back. But losing still sucked. They were competitors and their main goal was to win. They would try harder at their next game.

CHAPTER 17      THE ACCIDENT

The players were a happy bunch and on a natural high from their positive accomplishments of the last few weeks. They had one more game before the playoffs. Their excitement was palpable.

Since the players had a day off some of them decided to rent a minibus to visit Santa Fe. One of them went to the airport and rented it. He figured the big guys would appreciate the extra room. He picked up the players from the apartment complex and they headed out for a day of leisure in the State's capital. They had done some homework and were looking forward to visiting the oldest part of town, famous for its Plaza, shops, galleries and churches. One wanted to visit the famous staircase in the Loretto Chapel, another the Georgia O'Keefe Museum, and the rest just wanted to walk around the nation's oldest state capital and discover some delicious New Mexican food.

They headed north on I-25 and were as excited as schoolboys on a field trip. Ten minutes later, however, their enthusiasm collapsed and their journey was abruptly cut short. On the southbound lane the driver of a tractor-trailer gasped when his heart started beating furiously to the point and the blood flow to his brain was so drastically reduced that he lost consciousness. He collapsed onto the steering wheel, his weight pushing his legs forcefully down putting greater pressure on his foot on the gas pedal. The truck swerved uncontrollably and very fast from its lane, barreled across the median wildly and into the northbound lane. The players' vehicle was in the right place at the wrong time. The eighteen-wheeler smashed into the side of the van.

No one saw it coming. They were hit with such force that the minibus was thrown sideways and up into the air, then rolled several times very fast until it landed on its roof and finally skidded to a stop off the side of the highway. The truck's front end was totally pushed in and mangled. The entire trailer lay on its side across the lanes of the northbound road. Every car, in both directions, came to a screeching stop. Miraculously no other vehicles were involved. Passengers rushed out of their cars and hastily ran to help. Police and first responders were quickly on the scene. They all dreaded and cringed at the thought of the victims' condition and what they would see.

Oliver was the one who got the call.

"Yes, speaking," he answered the person asking for him. He listened for a few moments and for the first time in his life literally felt his heart skip a beat. "What? WHAT?" He repeated incredulously. "I understand, thank you very much, Officer," he said to the policeman, trying to stay as calm as possible.

Maxine, who was making brunch in the kitchen, detected the anxiety in his voice. "Oliver, what's wrong? What's happened?" She apprehensively asked, running up to him. His face was as pale as she had ever seen on a person.

Oliver looked at her with piteous eyes and held up an

index finger. He was calling William and she would hear.

Dezba and William were having a late breakfast at a restaurant in town when his cell rang.

"Hey, Oliver, what's up?"

"Will, there's been an accident. All I know is a bunch of our guys were heading to Santa Fe for some R&R and an eighteen-wheeler plowed into them."

Maxine's hand flew to her mouth to stifle a scream.

"Oh, my God! How bad?" William asked, the color draining from his face. Dezba immediately knew something was very wrong.

"The policeman told me it was pretty bad. No fatalities… so far," Oliver answered.

So far. The words pounded in William's head like a sledgehammer. He closed his eyes. It was his fault. He was the one who wanted a football team. They were there because of him. And if any of the men died… "Where are they?" He asked.

"They were transported to the hospital. A couple of them, the most critical, were airlifted by helicopter. I'll pick you up. I'm on my way."

"No, I'm at a restaurant in town with Dezba. Just tell me which one. We'll meet you there." A cold sweat ran down his spine.

"What's wrong?" Dezba asked worriedly as she watched William break into a sweat, even though the restaurant was on the cool side.

The two couples arrived at the same time and ran into the hospital building. Isaac had been told and was right behind them. Dezba grabbed a nurse and told her who they were and asked about the players.

"Yes, we've been expecting you. Come with me," she answered, leading them to the ICU floor where the men were being treated. She showed them a waiting area. "A doctor will be out shortly with an update."

"How much longer? Can you tell us something? Anything?" Dezba asked, wanting answers.

"I'm going back in now. Give me a few minutes. I'll either come out and tell you myself, or if the doctor has news, he'll be out first."

"Thank you very much," William said.

Other players and members of the staff started showing up. They wanted to know how their buddies were and prayed everyone would pull through. Too many had been hurt and that also triggered thoughts of the Natives being able to continue or not. They were thinking that maybe they wouldn't have a team anymore, at least for the remainder of the season.

A doctor came out to give the group an update on the condition of the patients. "I'm Doctor Grayson, you must be Mr. Quinn and you are Coach Hadley."

"That's right, Doctor. Please tell us…"

"Yes, most of them suffered broken bones. They, of course, will heal but the players will be side-lined for several months. A couple have concussions as well, and they, too, will be fine. One of them has a bad leg injury. Apparently his leg was pinned under some steel. It's amazing it was still attached. We're doing everything we can to save it."

The group was holding their breath as they listened attentively. They also noticed that the doctor was going from the somewhat 'best' case scenario to the worst.

The doctor continued: "The last two are being operated on. They came in critical condition."

"By helicopter?" Oliver asked.

"That's right."

"Will they make it, Doctor?"

"We're doing the best we can. I'll update you further as soon as we know more."

"Thank you, Doctor," William said. "Please, I know you're doing your very best, and if there is anything you need just name it."

"Yes, I will, Mr. Quinn," the doctor answered. He knew who William was and heard the man could move mountains.

William and Oliver went outside to get some fresh air. Instead of a little peace and quiet they were bombarded by reporters from what seemed every news media imaginable. The vans with their dishes on the roofs were camped outside and their lights flooded the area. This was the story of the year. Not only because they were a new NFL team who were showing great promise, but because now they had lost some of their best players in a horrific accident. Maybe there wouldn't even be a team. They were all hungry for the scoop. As humans they hoped the injuries were minimal, but as news reporters they knew the worse their condition the more newsworthy it would be. As the saying went 'the more it bleeds, the more it leads'.

"This is not the kind of publicity I had in mind," William said, cursing under his breath. "Where's Isaac?"

"Right behind you," the team PR man said. "I'll take care of the press as best I can."

"Thanks," William said.

Isaac was the ultimate pro. He spoke to the reporters for a few minutes, basically telling them that there certainly were bad injuries and that he would let them know as soon as the doctors told him more. They would have to be satisfied with that. Isaac would do his best to elevate the team and get the best results he could. He knew this was an unusual event and he would take advantage for the betterment of everyone concerned.

By the time Isaac finished with the media he knew the story would lead on every station in every city across the entire country, including Canada and Mexico and undoubtedly beyond the American continent as well. The world was not as familiar with American football, but everyone was interested in elite athletes, whether it was a sport they followed or not. They were, after all, unique talents. A devastating accident was unfortunately always popular. However, the outpouring of well-wishes and the coverage the New Mexico Natives were receiving was publicity that could never be bought. Although so many of the players were laid up no one really knew if the team would be able to go on. They were in a rather difficult predicament and the continuation of the team was uncertain. It was the hottest topic of the moment and Isaac didn't miss a single opportunity to promote them even more, albeit with prodigious tactfulness, whether they would be able to continue their season or not.

CHAPTER 18  NEW PLAYERS NEEDED

William, Oliver, George, Maxine and Dezba, who were the core of the tightknit little group, spent hours outside of the ORs waiting on the fate of their boys.

The surgeons came out one at a time from their individual operating rooms and gave them news of their patient's condition. The players' injuries ranged from severely broken bones to ruptured organs, to pieces of metal that had pierced their bodies, to concussions and brain bleeds. Fortunately, however, every single one pulled through and their status upgraded from critical to stable. Of course, there would be rehabilitation for all of them. Some would take longer than others to mend and recover. As for playing football, that was on an indefinite hold.

The little group headed for a cup of coffee. They sat glumly around a table in the hospital cafeteria. They were upset about the accident and the condition of the injured players.

"I'm very grateful we didn't lose anybody," Oliver said.

"Yeah, really," George agreed.

William had been thinking the same thing, but felt responsible.

"The team is down players. We lost most of our offensive line and all our legs," Oliver said.

"Legs?" Dezba asked.

"Kickers and punters. We don't have a single one left," George answered.

"Not one?" William asked.

"Not a single one," George repeated. "And most of our offensive linemen, running backs, wide receivers and tight ends are upstairs and out of commission."

"Basically, practically no offense and no kickers," Oliver added.

Cold sweat trickled down William's spine. The dream was falling apart. But the man wasn't where he was in life without the incredible drive he possessed. "There has to be a way," William said slowly.

"And we were doing so damned good!" George moaned. "We only had one more game before the playoffs!"

"And we probably would have been present," Oliver lamented.

For the next two days the little group worked furiously, fueled by the crumbling of their dream and the drive to keep it alive. Caffeine also helped. By the end of the second day they sat down in William's office around a conference table.

"How did we do?" William asked.

"I called every guy who tried out and didn't make the cut. They've either moved on, or aren't interested," George answered.

"All of them?"

"Yep, all of them. There weren't that many really. And then of course you have the superstitious ones."

"You mean the accident?" William asked incredulously.

"Uh, huh. Bad mojo or whatever."

"Their loss."

"That's what I said."

"Well, there's a couple of college teams, can we find anything in there?" William asked.

"It's worth a shot. We're desperate."

"George, you're a magician. If anybody can find players it's you."

"Don't know about that this time around."

"Uh, gentlemen," Dezba's little voice said, "maybe I can help."

"Oh, Dezba, that's very kind of you. Please don't tell me you want to try out, darlin'," George said.

She laughed good-heartedly, the idea never having even occurred to her. "No, no, but I know some guys that might want to. They're uh… a little different, but great athletes and good guys."

"One thing I know about you, Dezba, is that you seem to always find everything we need. I'm willing to try," William said. "What about you, guys?"

Oliver hadn't said much during their meeting. He was trying very hard not to feel defeated. "Bring them on," he answered.

George looked at his friend. Oh, boy, the man really was desperate.

"How about I set it up in the training facility for eight o'clock tomorrow morning?" Dezba asked.

"Sounds like a plan," Oliver answered.

Dezba immediately pulled out her phone from her jacket and started dialing. The first person she called was her brother.

"Hey, Sis, what's up?" The deep voice asked.

"Ahiga, I need your help."

"Are you alright? Is Neil okay?"

"Yes, I'm fine, and so is Neil, but I need you to help me with something.

"Name it," he said. Ahiga would hold up the world for his sister, or die trying. She was the only family he had and she had provided for both of them since she was a teenager. Their parents had died in a drunk driving related accident and Dezba had taken over the household and cared for her five year old brother. Her dream had been to go to college and get a degree in business and economics, but that hadn't been possible until Ahiga was older. She had juggled being a mother, father and big sister while providing food, shelter and being a family for her younger sibling. Ahiga hadn't been the best student in school—he didn't like it very much—but he was a strong boy and quite the handyman. He always helped his community with some sort of construction work. The neighbors would give him what little money they could and he was grateful and very proud every time he presented his earnings to his hard-working sister. Every time he did, her smile would light up his day. By the time he was a teenager and graduated high school he had grown to be a giant, standing almost seven feet tall. Ahiga would use his body well in the construction jobs in the city and the laborious work only made him stronger. By then he made enough for both himself and his sister and Dezba could go to college. Thankfully, she earned a scholarship and attended the University of New Mexico. At thirty years old she wasn't the youngest student anymore, but she didn't care. She was pursuing her dreams and wouldn't stop until she achieved her goal. While she slept her subconscious visions confirmed she would be successful in her path.

"What is it you need?" Ahiga asked her sister.

"Meet me at the Natives' practice facility at eight o'clock tomorrow morning," Dezba said.

"I'll be there."

Dezba's next call was to Delmar Johnson, an assistant coach on the UNM track team.

"It's me, Delmar speakin'," he sing-songed in a Jamaican accent.

"Hi, Delmar, it's Dezba. I have a question for you."

"What is it, my pretty?"

"Well," she started slowly, "I think the world should know what a brilliant athlete you are."

"Absolutely."

"Right?"

"Yes, right."

"What do you know about football?"

"American football?"

"Uh, uh."

"Catch the ball and go to the big yellow post and make a goal. What is it you want to know?"

Dezba told him her idea. The answer he gave her was a cacophonous laugh that seemed to last forever.

"Oh, my pretty, you are so funny, but I will gladly try to help you out. I'll meet you in the morning." He would never disappoint a beautiful woman, even if her idea was completely crazy. "Bless up!"

"You have a good day, too, and thank you."

When Dezba hung up with Delmar she called a French pastry shop. She had a sweet tooth and was very familiar with the staff who worked there. The store was close to UNM's campus and she was known to stop in at least twice a week.

"*Café de l'Ouest, bonjour!*" The voice on the line said.

"Jacques?"

"*Oui*, this is Jacques, who is this?"

"It's Dezba."

"Ah, Dezba, how are you?"

"I'm good. I need your help."

"Of course! Today I have delicious *croissants, éclairs, madeleines* covered with *chocolat*, beautiful *macarons, mille-feuilles*, what you call Napoleon..." Jacques was very passionate about his creations.

"Oh, yes, that's sounds delicious and I will definitely need a box, but I have something else very special in mind."

"Tell me," he said quickly, thrilled with the prospect of a challenge.

Dezba did. When she finished no sound came from the other end of the call. "Jacques? Are you there?"

"I am, *ma petite*," Jacques answered. He had expected anything that contained flour or eggs, but not grass and uniforms. The athlete in him, however, was just as excited as the pastry chef.

"Well?" Dezba asked anxiously.

"I thought you needed a special order. This is definitely something special. *Oui*, I will be there tomorrow morning."

"Oh, Jacques, thank you so much."

"My pleasure. Now, this problem of yours, maybe I can help a little more."

"If you're thinking wonderful pastries, absolutely!"

Jacques laughed. "Of course, that would help everything, but I was thinking maybe I can bring two friends with me. They are athletes too."

"What kind of athletes?"

"Very good ones, I promise."

"Sure, why not? What are their names?"

"Bartolomeo and Zacharias, but everybody calls him Zorba."

"Okay, see you tomorrow, and thank you again."

A short while later Dezba walked into William's office. The man looked up and smiled. This woman made him glow. It was a sensation he had never experienced before, and he loved it.

"Are you really busy?" She asked.

"Nothing that can't wait. What did you have in mind?"

"I need to go to one of the casinos on the outskirts of town."

"You want to go play?"

"No," she giggled, "I want to talk to some interesting guys I heard were in town for a few days. Maybe I can convince them to try out tomorrow. Want to come?"

"Sure!" Of course he wanted to spend time with her and everything he was doing could be done by phone anyway. "Let's go," he said, standing up. He grabbed the keys off his desk and followed her out of his office.

"I'll drive," Dezba said.

"Okay." William handed her the keys.

They took I-25 north toward the casino.

"So who are these guys?" William asked.

"They're actually here for a demonstration, kind of a show, you know to introduce the public to their craft which originated in Japan."

"They're artists?"

"In a way they are, but more athletes. They're not from here, or the continental U.S. They're very interesting and I talked to them. They're expecting us." Dezba stopped. She knew this was going to be an incredibly long shot, but they were desperate.

"Sounds like geishas from a Japanese Kabuki theater, or whatever the male version is, if there even is such a thing."

This was so far opposite from what they were going to see that Dezba thought she would die laughing right there in the middle of the highway. William looked at her. The woman was laughing so hard tears ran down her cheeks. It was absolutely impossible for her to speak and explain her bout of hilarity. The woman was sure she had never laughed so hard in her life. Thankfully she was driving and focused on the road. William was concentrating on her. She was so endearing and wistful he understood that he was falling under her spell, and he wanted more.

A few minutes later they arrived at their destination. They left the car for the valet and entered the casino.

"Now, Will, I wasn't going to say anything, but I feel bad."

"What do you mean?"

"Well, obviously we aren't going to meet lovely geishas."

William chuckled. "Yeah, I figured that, with you laughing your head off in the car and all."

"Right," she giggled, remembering her bout. "The guys we're going to meet are big guys, and they're triplets."

"How nice." William wasn't sure how to react. Where was she going with this?

"I'm pretty sure they'll be open to try out tomorrow morning, all three of them."

"Big guys sound like the right formula. You said they're here for a show, what do they do?"

"They're sumo wrestlers from Samoa."

It was William's turn. At first he just stared blankly trying to comprehend the image in his head that was transforming lovely geishas to hulk-like sumo wrestlers. And then he started laughing so hard Dezba thought he would have a heart attack.

"Are you alright?" She asked, laughing with him. "Now you know why I just about died when you said geishas."

William could only nod vigorously as he fervently tried to catch his breath. He couldn't remember when he had laughed so hard, or felt so good, especially in the company of a woman. Oh, laughing truly was the best medicine in the world, and of course with Dezba having entered his life, this moment in time was perfection.

She stared at him. His eyes seemed to shine differently when he looked at her and she wondered if her own eyes glowed the same way. She was sure her heart did. "Well, ready to meet them?" She asked.

"I'll try my very best."

"I have no doubt you'll do just fine."

CHAPTER 19  NEW PLAYERS' TRYOUTS

Oliver and George watched a handsome six-foot-four, long-limbed man walking toward them.

"Pretty boy, isn't he, with his mustache and all. I'll wager the girls love this one," George said.

"I would bet on that, too. Reminds me of a black Burt Reynolds with dreadlocks," Oliver answered.

George chuckled. "Hopefully he's just as good a football player."

"Let's find out more about him."

As he stopped in front of them George asked: "Your name?"

"Delmar Johnson, mon." Even though he had said 'man', it sounded more like 'mon'.

"Jamaican?" Oliver asked.

"Did my accent give it away?"

"Something like that. My notes here say you're a runner."

"My specialty is the 110 meter hurdles, mon."

Oliver liked that. That meant that he was surely fast and could jump over another player. "So, you're a runner."

"I can run you a 110 if you want, mon."

"That's nice, even though that's about twenty yards longer than a football field. But are you fast?"

"I am that. I was on the Jamaican Olympic team… but never got to the games."

"What happened? Did you get hurt?"

"Naw, mon, I got caught enjoyin' a reefer."

"Well, that's a good way to fuck up your career and your future," Oliver said, perturbed at the stupidity.

"'Tis true, mon."

"And now? Do you still indulge?"

"Well, you know," Delmar chuckled.

"I'll be honest with you. There's nothing I hate more than drugs, but I'm going to let you try out and we'll talk about that later. And how did you end up in Albuquerque?"

"I had to leave Jamaica in a hurry, mon. I remembered a show on television a few years ago called In Plain Sight. It had to do with witness protection program and I thought now there's a city people wouldn't look for me."

"And they were looking for you why?"

"I had a disagreement with the chief of police, mon."

"How serious?"

"Very serious to him. He didn't like me dating his pretty daughter," he sighed. "Oh, her lips were like cherry wine and her body was as beautiful and tasty as smooth chocolate ganache."

Oliver tried to stay serious, but the man was naturally endearing. "Was she the love of your life?"

"Don't get me wrong, mon, I love all women, any size, any color. But Rosalie was more than just a woman, she was part of my soul, mon."

"And also the daughter of the police chief."

"Yeah, mon. I don't know if it was just me, or any man, but she was hands off. I know she loved me, just like I loved her."

Oliver wasn't sure why he let Delmar ramble on, but

he was getting a kick out of the Jamaican. Perhaps he was just trying to lighten up the stress of the past few days.

"I understand," Oliver said, thinking of his own daughter. "And how did you get in to the States?"

"You mean am I legal, mon?"

"Yes."

"No worries, mon, I was born in New York, but my Papi he took me back to the island when my mother died. I grew up mainly with my granny."

"Alright, let's see what you can do. I want you to run a forty-yard dash."

"Not the length of the field?"

"No, just forty yards, as fast as you can."

"Okay."

George showed him the starting point and Delmar headed toward it. He waved to him. "When I say go, you go. Ready?"

Delmar shook his hands a little and then his legs. "Ready!"

"And GO!"

Delmar did and both Oliver and George started their stopwatches. They clicked them when the sprinter crossed the line.

"4.8!" George exclaimed.

Delmar walked back to them. "I was just warmin' up. I'm going again," he said.

Oliver and George looked at each other and grinned. "Okay, go right ahead," Oliver said.

Delmar did. When they looked at their stopwatches both George and Oliver saw 4.3.

"Shit! This boy can run," George said.

Oliver called him back. "Delmar, tell me, isn't the best 110 hurdles around thirteen seconds?"

"That would be right."

"And what was your best?"

"12.92."

Oliver whistled. "Isn't that a world record?"

"Well, almost. Aries Merritt holds that one at 12.80."

"Okay, Delmar, now go with George over to Neil Howard, our quarterback. He's going to throw you some passes."

"No worries, mon."

After ten minutes, George went back to Oliver. "You're not going to like this."

"What's wrong?" Oliver asked.

"You know how Delmar said 'no worries'"?

"Uh, huh."

"Well, you should."

"Why? Is he stoned or something?"

"Worse!"

"What?"

"He can run like the wind, but he can't catch a fucking ball. Reminded me of those special effects in the movies when people walk through walls like water," he grumbled.

George's news didn't make Oliver very happy. "That bad?" He asked.

"Neil kept throwing him perfect spirals, but they all slipped through his hands.

"Well, I have faith. We'll just keep working on it."

"If you say so," George said shaking his head. The Jamaican was a gazelle, but he couldn't hold on to a ball for shit.

"Okay, who's next?"

"That guy right there." George waived a man over to them.

A stocky man of five feet eight inches walked over. They could see the muscles in his body were rock hard and his face was movie-star handsome, although his nose was far from perfect and crooked, a tell-tale of brokenness, and of more than once. It didn't mar his good looks though, rather it gave him an interesting and mysterious flair. The man stopped in front of them.

"Hi, what's your name?" George asked.

"Jacques Dupont," he said with a French accent.

"Canadian? French?" Oliver asked.

"Yes, from *France*."

Oliver and George watched as he did the forty-yard dash. Jacques was quick on the take-off and a fast runner, not as good as Delmar of course and no one would be, but they were pleased. As with Delmar he and George went over to Neil to catch some passes. The older man watched but wondered at his technique.

"Hey, where did you learn to catch like that?" George asked.

"Is something wrong?"

"No, just curious."

"In France. I'm a rugby player."

Ah, now it made sense, George thought to himself. He's quick, it's tough to get the ball from him and he can barrel through the obstacles. Neil threw the ball at Jacques again. The Frenchman had a peculiar way of catching it. He and several other players ran a play. After a couple of yards he saw an opposing player ready to tackle him so he threw it to a player behind him who didn't expect it and dropped it.

"No, no, this isn't rugby, you have to hold on to it."

"But they were going to pile on top of me and block the ball."

"Well, that's part of American football, so you just have to avoid that."

"I see," Jacques answered. He didn't.

Did he? George liked the Frenchman. With a little

direction and practice he could work out. The older man went back to Oliver.

"The guy's pretty good, used to be a rugby player. He's quick and tough. I think we can make him work."

"Good. I like athletes that have played different sports. It gives them an edge and comes in handy. The body knows more tricks and has additional and different muscle memory. Okay. Who's next?"

George waved another man over. "Baki?" He said.

"Bacci, *Ba-chee*, Bartolomeo Bacci," the man corrected him, "Bacci, like kisses, like the chocolate candy," he said with typical Italian enthusiasm. "You can call me Bacci or Bartolomeo or Barto."

Another European, Oliver thought, getting more frustrated and desperate. "What do you do?"

"I teach physics to students. I am a teacher."

"Do you play football?" Oliver asked.

"Of course. I was the goal-keeper for my team, eh, in Italy. I was the best of course."

"Of course," George said.

Oliver and George were like balloons slowly deflating. What were they going to do with a goal-keeper?

George was holding a football. Bartolomeo looked at it, intrigued. George thought he was going to die on the spot where he stood as he realized the Italian man probably never touched a ball that wasn't round.

They tried him out anyway. He was a good runner, not as fast as Delmar or even Jacques, but good enough. However, when George threw a ball at him when he wasn't really paying attention Bartolomeo managed to catch it with lightning speed. He had hands like an octopus. Oliver threw three balls at him at the same time. He didn't drop any and was enthused as he jumped to grab them: "*Si, si! Perfetto!* Again, again!" He could have caught them in his sleep and quickly figured out how to catch the oblong ball. George gave him some pointers and all three of them were happy with the results.

Since the Italian was a soccer player he could also kick, something they desperately needed as their punters and kickers were laid up. Of course he didn't know anything about *football Americano* and asked the coaches: "Where should I kick your balls?" Oliver and George almost covered their genitals but understood what Bart meant. He continued: "Where should it land? Behind the goal posts? Through the posts? Under?"

George groaned.

Oliver called an assistant. "Do you have any cans?"

"Plastic bottles?"

"That'll work. I need you to place them for me on the field," Oliver said and instructed the man on where to put them. The assistant put the bottles near the end zone and in the spots Oliver wanted Bartolomeo to kick the ball to.

"Okay, Bacci, I want you to kick the ball as close as you can to the bottles, but from the air. I don't want them to hit the grass first. *Capisce?*" Oliver asked.

"*Si, si, capisco!* But how close?"

"As close as possible."

"No problem. One ball to kick to get feel first, okay?" Bart said as he took a ball from George. He felt the ball, tossed it slightly up in the air to understand its weight and then dropped it onto one of his feet. He juggled it back and forth between them.

"He's never touched one of these," George whispered to Oliver.

"Mmm, got that," Oliver whispered back. "Maybe his physics background might help."

George rolled his eyes toward the sky.

Bartolomeo kicked the ball. "Ah, okay, no problem. I understand this ball now."

Oliver and George raised their eyebrows. An assistant handed Bart another ball. Bart took it and kicked it. It landed on one of the plastic bottles just the way they asked.

"Nice." George said, keeping his enthusiasm in check. Was that a fluke or could he do that again?

The assistant handed him more footballs. Bart kicked them in quick succession. Each one landed on top of a bottle.

"Is good, *si?*"

"Oh, *si*, Bart! Can I call you Bart?" George asked.

"*Si, si, assolutamente!*"

"Now try to kick a ball in the corner right in front of the orange pylon and make the ball spin out of the field as soon as it hits. Practice that."

"Okay, *va bene*, no problem."

Bartolomeo kicked a couple of balls. After a few minutes he knew precisely where and how to hit them and did exactly what the coaches wanted. Oliver and George grinned, perhaps their biggest smiles since the news of the accident.

The coaches kept watching. Bart was a fast learner and apparently his physics was coming in handy too.

"He's looking good," George said."

Bart came up to them. He was excited with this new game. "I have question for you. Can I just kick it through the goal posts and make goal?"

"You mean a touchdown?"

"*Si*, six points, no?"

"Yes, a touchdown is six points, and no, it would not count."

"Why not?"

"Because the only reason you are kicking the ball is to give it to the other team."

"Give the ball to the other team? That makes no sense. I am supposed to give it to *my* team."

"Yeah, uh, no. This is American football."

"Is backwards, no?"

George didn't answer. It was a lost cause. But he liked the Italian and he would do everything he could to teach him as much as possible.

Oliver and George continued trying out other players.

"Okay, who's next?" Oliver asked.

George looked at his paper and then just pointed to it. "Him. It's a Greek name," he said flatly.

"Jeeesus," Oliver said as he tried to read it, which was impossible.

The short man walked over to them. He couldn't have been more than five feet five and a hundred sixty pounds soaking wet. Oliver and George's very first thought was if this man played football he would be crushed or broken like a stick in the first play. They were impressed, however, by the bulging muscles on his body, especially his arms.

"Man, with those arms and legs if the guy was just a little shorter he'd be square," George whispered.

"Uh, huh."

The man stopped in front of the two coaches.

"Hello," he said cheerfully.

"Hi," Oliver said, "your name?" Both he and George were waiting for this one.

"Zacharias Papagrammatikopoulos. It's Greek."

"Right, got that." Oliver answered.

"Everybody calls me Zorba."

In what position could this little guy be useful, they

wondered. He would last about as long as it would take to make souvlaki out of him. Maybe special teams?

"Alright, do you have a specialty in something?" Oliver asked, wondering why this little Greek wanted to be on a football team. By now he wondered if Dezba had probably gone overseas to find players. So far they had a Jamaican, a Frenchman, an Italian and now a Greek.

"Oh, yes, I am a gymnast and a dancer," he answered proudly. Anything Greeks did, they did with great pride, and were of course the best at it, or had invented it.

Oliver and George lifted their eyebrows.

"Very nice. What kind of dancing?" Oliver asked, cringing at the thought that he might say ballet, although those guys were incredible athletes too.

"Greek dances, of course!" He immediately lifted his arms and posed as if he were going to start dancing.

"Yeah, that's great, Zorba. That's good. Why don't we start you on some dashes," George said.

"Of course."

The Greek man did as they asked. He was a good sprinter, caught the balls well and held on tight. Probably from running toward the vault and hanging on for dear life on the bars or rings, Oliver thought.

They ran him through the footwork grids and whistled when the man's feet were barely visible. They had never seen faster feet in their lives. Zorba went through the tires and obstacles without stepping on anything he wasn't supposed to.

They tried him in a play. Neal passed him the ball and he easily squeezed between the opposing players like butter. By the time everybody realized he had gotten passed them, the others couldn't catch up to him. As he arrived in the end zone and after supposedly scoring a touchdown, the man did a back flip and struck a 'Zorba the Greek' pose. The other players just stared and then clapped.

Oliver and George looked at each other and raised their eyebrows. Very interesting, they thought.

They tried another play and this time Zorba got crunched between two much, much bigger guys. Oliver and George feared the worst, but the short man was undoubtedly made of rubber and could take as much punishment as anyone.

"Okay, he's in too," Oliver said. "Who's next?"

George poked his elbow into Oliver's ribs. "I think I'm seeing triple and I haven't had a drink yet."

"What are you talking about?" Oliver asked. He was tired and in no mood for jokes he couldn't understand, at least not at the moment.

"Take a look."

Oliver did and then made a strange sound, something between a gasp, a groan and laughter. He now understood what George was referring to. Heading toward them were the Samoan triplets. He remembered William mentioning something about them and now it was registering.

Oliver could have sworn the earth shook as the six foot six, 360-pound sumo wrestlers walked up to them. They looked exactly alike, the only difference was a bandana of a different color around their foreheads. They also sported the traditional *chonmage*, the sumo wrestlers' hairstyle with the shaved pate and a thick oiled ponytail that looped back up to the bald area into a topknot. What was once an Edo-era Samurai hairstyle meant to hold a head protector now would perhaps be tucked into an American football helmet. They stopped in front of the coaches. Standing next to each other they made a perfect wall. Oliver pictured the fans in the stands with their signs of D and the little fence next to it. Defense indeed.

"Gentlemen, welcome," he said.

"Coach," one of them acknowledged.

"I hear you're sumo wrestlers from the beautiful island of Samoa."

"That's right," the same one answered.

"And what are your names?"

"I'm Toma, this is Ualesi and he's Viliamu. Our last name is Vaimoa," he answered.

"And you're of course triplets."

"We are."

Oliver looked at the other two who hadn't uttered a word. "Do you guys speak?"

"Sometimes," Ualesi said, "but Toma is the oldest and does most of the talking."

"I thought you were triplets," Oliver asked.

"We're each five minutes apart," Viliamu, the youngest said.

"I see. Okay. So you're professional sumo wrestlers," Oliver continued.

The three of them nodded.

"Sumo is a traditional Japanese sport. How did you get into it?"

"Samoans love wrestling and there are a lot of big guys on the island. The three of us happen to be pretty good at it."

"Have you ever played football?" George asked.

"In high school, in Samoa."

"That's great," George said, thrilled that he wouldn't have to explain how the damn game worked. He'd had enough of that with the previous guys. "What position?"

"Defense," Toma said.

Ya think? George wanted to say. Instead he guided them toward the bag blocking drills. "Okay, let's see what you guys can do."

"Well?" Oliver asked George when he was finished with the Samoans.

"Best we'll get. We'll make it work," he said with false confidence.

"Great."

"Hi, Coach," Ahiga said, walking up behind them.

When they turned around they looked straight up to see the man's face.

"Hey, Ahiga, good to see you."

"You too, Coach."

"George, this is Ahiga, Dezba's brother."

"Nice to meet you." This was one big boy, he thought. He almost extended his hand, almost, but then decided not to. He wondered if this giant, who was even bigger than Gronkowski, could move even half as fast. The man was just too big for football. George laughed inwardly at his last statement. He didn't think anyone could ever be 'too big' for this sport. He could tell by the way the man walked that he was as strong as a bull but wasn't light on his feet.

"What brings you around?" Oliver asked.

"Dezba said you might need some help with the team. Seems you lost quite a few players."

"Yes, unfortunately. At least they'll all pull through. Tell me, you play sports? Basketball maybe? You've obviously got the height."

"I did, but I couldn't run too much, or fast enough."

"You play any football, Ahiga?" George asked. "By the way, does your name mean anything? I know it's tradition with Native Americans."

Ahiga smiled. "It means 'he fight'. I can do that. I played defense for a while in high school, but not for long," he answered.

"How come?"

"I couldn't control my strength," he whispered somewhat ashamed.

"That's because those idiots didn't know how to teach you properly," George said, feeling protective toward the big man. He could tell Ahiga was a typical 'teddy bear'—humble, cuddly and careful not to hurt anyone with his strength—until someone was being a bully, where he would then go into 'protective mode' and his temper would flare. That could come in handy, George pondered.

"Well, let's give you a try, shall we? If you would like to, that is," Oliver said.

"I just came to help out my sis, but I really would love to play, Coach."

Oliver thought he would put him in the Center position. It was the spot of one of the most special players and he just had a feeling, in addition to Ahiga's size, of course. Just like George he figured out he was a 'teddy bear'. Plays and ideas were already forming in his mind. With his long arms and legs it would take the opponent a sliver of extra time to get to the QB, which could make all the difference in the world. He hoped he was right.

"Great, this time let's try you in a different position. We're going for offense."

The big man stared. No one had every told him that he could play on that line. Just what did the coach have in store for him?

The tryouts were almost over and Oliver stared at the men on the field. If he didn't know any better he would have sworn he was watching a live cartoon. Zorba was carrying the ball and weaving, literally, through the legs of the Samoan Sumos, doing a great impersonation of the

Road Runner. The triplets were about as successful as Wile E. Coyote with an added combined thousand pounds. Jacques was running with the ball toward the end zone and threw the ball behind him, a typical rugby move, as another player was close to tackling him. There was, of course, no one there. The Frenchman stopped and threw up his hands.

Oliver didn't know if he should cry or laugh. He decided they'd all had enough for the day. He blew on his whistle and called them in.

"Okay, go clean up, men," Oliver said. "Oh, Delmar, a word?" he beckoned to him.

The Jamaican went over to him. "What's up, mon?"

"I would like you on the team, Delmar, however, I am warning you that if I either smell or find out that you looked or touched anything remotely related to pot, or any kind of drug not only will you be cut from the team but I'm going to tell Zorba to show the Samoans and Ahiga how to make a shish kebab out of you.

Delmar looked at him. *Was the man serious or just a little bit crazy*, he asked himself. *Me tinks a little of both*, he concluded. "You have a deal, mon."

"Coach."

"Ya, mon, Coach," Delmar repeated. "Mi wi see yuh."

The men shook hands. They would both keep their promise. Neil despised narcotics in any form unless it was medicinal for patients. Delmar had given his word and the man was only as good as his word. Besides, he was friends with Bart, Zorba and Jacques and he would never embarrass his buddies.

When they were gone George looked at his friend. "I guess that means I'll see ya."

"I think it does."

"Oliver, how can we make two guys into one?" The older man asked.

"You mean Delmar and Bart? One's speed, the other's hands?"

"Exactly."

"I know," Oliver sighed.

Oliver called William. They would meet for dinner to talk about the try-outs.

CHAPTER 20  LOCKER ROOM

| | | | | | | | | | | | | | | | | | | | | | | | | | | | | | | | | | | | | | | | | | | | | | | | | | | | |

The young men came off the field from their tryouts and entered the locker room. They didn't care how they smelled, and reek they did. It couldn't be helped with so much perspiration covering them from the day's heat and exertion. But they were happy. Those who had been previously cut were given a second chance. The newcomers, including the ones who hadn't grown up with football, were just as excited. They were athletes, possibly from different sports, but they were all part of a club, an elite club that used their minds and bodies with a God-given talent they lovingly and proudly shared with the world. Right at the moment they were oblivious to anything but the dream that could possibly be theirs. They would know in the next twenty-four hours if their life was changed forever or not.

Bart, Zorba, Jacques and Delmar were complaining about their helmets as they were taking them off. None of them wore head protection in their respective sports.

Porca miseria, I don't like this protection at all!" Bart moaned

"*Ah, oui,* I know what you mean! All day it has been bothering me too!" Jacques agreed.

"Yes, same here," Zorba added.

"Unfortunately it's part of the uniform and we have to

wear the damn thing, mon," Delmar sighed.

"Don't worry, guys, you'll get used to it. You did great out there today," one of the players said.

"So what's your name, Frenchie?" Another player asked. He seemed a little rough on the edges.

"Jacques Dupont."

"Jack Dupont," he said, emphasizing the T.

"It is Jacques, not Jack, and you do not pronounce the T in Dupont, like *bon appetit*, no T, and *blanc*, you know like white wine or *beurre* blanc, no C. In the French language you do not pronounce the last letter in words. There are exceptions of course, but very few."

"Okay, Frenchie, we get it, MonsieuR DuponT," he said, emphasizing the R and the T at the end of the words.

"It is *Monsieur*, no R, *bande de cons*."

"Band what?"

"You are nothing but a group of assholes…" Jacques started, but quickly stopped when the big guys starting coming his way, "…but you have big hearts, *mes amis*, my friends, my teammates."

They laughed and smacked him gently on the ass with their towels.

"*Les Americains*, they are crazy and very little savoir vivre, but good-hearted," Jacques sighed.

"So, pretty boy, you do okay with the ladies, even though you're not very tall?"

Jacques smiled. "Look, and maybe learn." He made a fist in front of him. He stuck his thumb straight out toward himself and his index finger toward the ceiling. "You see my fingers?" He asked.

"Yeah, kind of looks like you'll holding a gun toward the ceiling."

"Now, watch." Jacques turned his hand slowly until

the fingers were reversed, as if he were pointing a gun. "It is not how tall you are, *mon ami.*"

The other men had gotten wind of what was going on and they now laughed good-heartedly. They also wondered if the Frenchman was talking about himself, as he had clearly intonated. They found out soon enough when they hit the showers. The man hadn't been lying.

"Hey, triplets, where are you from?" Delmar asked.

"From Samoa," they answered together.

"That's between Hawaii and New Zealand, right?"

"That's right. And you?" Toma asked.

"I'm from an island too, Jamaica, mon."

Most of the men in the locker room were big, with big bodies and big arms. One of them followed Zorba with his eyes. After a few minutes he went up to him.

"Damn, boy, you got some arms on you! Pretty good for a short guy," he said.

"I'm not as tall as you, but I am just as strong and I am sure much more flexible."

"Oh yeah?"

"Yes." Zorba put his hands on the floor, did a handstand and started push-ups.

"Okay, not bad, you probably got us there, but that doesn't show us how strong you really are."

"No problem, I'll show you." Zorba took the linebacker's hands and lifted his arms until they were straight in front of him. "Can you keep them there even if I hang on them?"

The other players who had been watching the little tête-à-tête started laughing.

"Of course I can!"

"Great. Hang on." Zorba walked under one arm and stood between the big man's forearms, his back toward the man's chest. He put his hands on them and lifted himself as if they were parallel bars. His arms were straight and locked and he very slowly lifted his legs in front of him and pointed his toes until his body was a perfect L.

"Hold tight now," Zorba said.

"Don't worry about me, I got you."

Zorba, still in the same L position, slightly pushed the big man's arms out until they slightly parted and Zorba pushed his own arms until he ended up in an iron cross.

"Shit, man, look at his biceps, they're like melons!" another player said, duly impressed.

Zorba continued. From the position he was in he pulled their arms back to their original position. He slowly moved his torso forward and then smoothly lifted his legs until they pointed straight toward the ceiling. "How are you doing, big man?" He asked.

"I'm good."

Zorba looked at him. They were facing each other now, but their faces were upside down. "I'm going to do a back flip and dismount. Can you hold me?"

"Absolutely," he said, although his arms were starting to slightly shake. Zorba had of course felt that, which is why he asked.

"Good. Here I go." And he did. He pushed hard on the forearms which gave him a little lift, tucked his legs into his chest, rotated backward and landed on his feet.

The players who had been watching all clapped. Some smacked Zorba on his back.

The Greek man, as he had with the coaches, struck up a 'Zorba' pose and then bowed.

CHAPTER 21  UNCOVENTIONALS

William, Oliver, George, Isaac, Maxine and Dezba sat around a table eating dinner in a restaurant. It was an almost daily ritual where everyone was brought up to speed on all the events, including the status of the players from the accident. On this day the main subject was centered on the tryouts.

Oliver pulled out a notepad from his pocket. "Okay, here are the guys we checked out today. I think they'll be able to help the team and we'll have enough players to get through the season. We're still short a few players but we can double them up on occasion, such as send them over to special teams when needed."

"I'm glad we still have apartments available for the new players," William said. "As far as the men you saw today, if you want them, you've got them. That's your department, Oliver, and you know you have carte blanche."

"Thanks, Will."

"Any details I should know before I meet them?"

"They're a different bunch, not quite what we usually get in NFL tryouts, but they're magnificent athletes and have a quality or talent that could serve us well."

"Such as?"

Oliver looked at his notepad and then at William and

said: "Such as Delmar Johnson, former member of the Jamaican Olympic 110-meter hurdle team."

"Wow, so he can run," Will said, impressed.

"Absolutely, and jump," Oliver answered.

"But can't catch for shit," George muttered inaudibly under his breath.

"Then we have Jacques Dupont, one of Europe's premier rugby players and possibly the best in France."

"Does he know American football?"

"It's coming along."

George rolled his eyes toward the ceiling, but he acknowledged: "He's clever, a quick thinker and great athlete."

"Sounds good. What did he do before this?"

"He's a pastry chef in town," Dezba said.

"Oh, I like that. If he doesn't work out on the field we'll hire him to make French pastries."

"There is a slight problem. He can't be seen by too many people," Oliver said.

William stared at him and asked: "How does that work? Football is watched by millions of people, and Isaac is making very sure of that."

"I am," the public relations man said.

"Yeah, I think maybe only you can fix the problem, Will."

"I can? And just what is the problem?"

"He likes women, a lot. Good Frenchman you know."

"Okay, I don't see anything wrong with that."

"Well, he got mixed up with the wife of a French minister. The said husband got really pissed off and supposedly put a hit out on him."

"Seriously?"

"What I've heard."

"Don't all Frenchmen, especially the politicians, have

mistresses on the side?" William asked.

Maxine chimed in. "Well, they're known to, but I'm guessing they don't much like it if the wife plays what their husbands think is *their* exclusive game. He also looks like a young Alain Delon, the French movie star."

"Probably why the Minister's wifey enjoyed herself," Dezba added.

"You don't say, ladies," William laughed.

"Hey, that's great for our lady fans," Isaac quickly added.

"This team is getting quite interesting. Beauties, every one of them," William groaned. "I'll see what I can do about his little problem."

"Uh, before the game."

"Of course," William agreed, already thinking that his uncle Frank would probably be the best person to talk to and get the problem resolved. He always knew someone who knew someone and of course he was the one William had called to fix the Neil Howard problem. From what his uncle reported the quarterback was completely clear of the loan sharks or any debt.

Oliver continued: "We also found a kicker, an Italian soccer goalie. He's pretty good."

"And he's cute too. Blond, blue eyes. Must be from northern Italy," Maxine added.

Oliver looked at her. A little jealousy tweaked his chest for a moment but he immediately realized there was nothing to be jealous of. The two of them were very much in love and there was no reason for either one of them not to trust the other. Besides, the way her eyes looked at him told him everything he needed to know— they had a special shine just for him.

"Sounds positive. Who else?" William said.

"Your Samoans sumos made the cut," Oliver

continued. "The triplets picked up the plays easily and they're quick."

"Running?" William asked, somehow doubting that.

"No, their reactions are quick and they're solid as mountains.

"That's our Geishas," Dezba said and giggled. William did too.

"Huh?" Oliver asked.

"Oh, nothing, long story, I'll tell you some other time. "I'm glad they're with us, they seem like nice guys."

"Well, Max, are they good looking too?" Oliver chuckled.

"Aw, of course our little Buddhas are cute. We have the best-looking team in the nation."

"I agree," Dezba said.

"Hey, maybe we should put out a calendar!" Isaac said enthusiastically.

"Isaac…" William started.

"I'm serious," he continued, already thinking that Neil Howard would be Mr. January, the first month.

"Well, maybe we can give the money to a worthwhile cause, like education," William said.

"From a calendar of half-naked men?" Oliver asked. "I presume, besides the face, they want to see some bulging muscles?"

"I'll work the angle," Isaac asserted. "Oh, yes!" He exclaimed, having another idea.

"Should I be afraid to ask?" William said.

"We will go international with it and it will give American football worldwide exposure and would help the NFL get the sport out there."

"Oh, they'll like that," George said.

"And not just one charity, but several!" Isaac said as his mind was already formulating details.

The little group laughed, but they also knew the PR man was amazing at manifesting his ideas.

"Okay, let's get back to the players. Any other I should know about?" William asked.

"Well, we have one more character, Zacharias Papa-g-something, better known as Zorba," Oliver said.

"Zorba? As in Kazantzakis' Cretan?" William asked.

"Uh, huh."

"What does he do? Dance?"

"Yup. Zorba has the fastest feet you've ever seen in your life. When he gets tackled and goes down it's won't be because of his feet," George said.

"Last, but definitely not least, we have a diamond in the rough—Ahiga," Oliver said.

"My brother?" Dezba asked.

"Absolutely. He's a big boy, and strong as hell, but his greatest asset is his mind." Oliver had everyone's attention, and only George knew how right his old friend was. He listened with a smile on his face as if he had won the lottery. "Yes," Oliver continued, "and Max, you are going to love him."

"Of course I am, he's Dezba's brother."

"Well, yes, but in addition he has a military mind!"

"Really!" Maxine said excitedly.

"Yes! He can read plays and retain them as if he had a photographic memory and figures out the opposition's moves in an instant. He is like a maestro of the offense. He's our new center. And he's a great snapper. He and Neil immediately clicked. He's got good hands."

"Well, they're big enough," Dezba said. She was on her second Cognac and was a little giddy.

"Dezba!" William mockingly scolded her. She was so damned cute, he thought.

"Well, he's seven feet tall!"

"Hey, is he a descendent of a Code Talker?" Isaac asked Dezba excitedly. He knew well of the valiant WWII Navajo Marines and wondered if that had anything to do with what Oliver called his 'military' mind.

"I don't think so. Not that I'm aware of," Dezba answered.

"That's a pity," Isaac said.

William looked around the table and said: "Well, we certainly have an interesting, unconventional and international group of players—from France, Italy, Greece, Jamaica and Samoa. We also have Max of course from England, Oliver and I have Irish roots, and last but definitely not least our beloved Native Americans including Dezba and Ahiga."

"Yup, we're the real deal, the original Americans," Dezba said giggling.

"Yes, we are from here and the rest of the world. And together we are one, yet unique."

"Don't you think Ahiga looks a little like the Natives' logo?" Dezba asked, on her way to getting quite tipsy.

The group enjoyed the rest of the evening with laughter, dessert and William's beloved Cognac.

CHAPTER 22  NEW PLAYERS' RESULTS

Maxine and Oliver were in bed after a long and stressful day and Oliver was pretty much passed out. She had been present at the tryouts and now her mind was going a million miles a minute. The inside of her brain probably looked like a laser show. Maxine was excited, and so many crazy plays were forming in her head that she couldn't sleep so she carefully slipped out of bed and returned with her laptop. She quietly sat up against the backboard and put the portable computer on her legs and searched the internet for sumo wrestling and rugby. She knew quite a bit about rugby since her brother Charles had played, but she studied both sports for several hours. By the time the rays of sun started winking through the curtains she smiled, completely satisfied with her research and her newly acquired knowledge. Not only did she want to help Jacques and the triplets but she thought that if she better understood their sport she could assist even more. As she was learning about the other sports her strategic mind had come up with some innovative plays.

She yawned, closed her computer and immediately fell asleep.

A couple of hours later Maxine heard Oliver walking around the apartment. She got out of bed and joined him.

"Good morning, Oli, how are you?"

"Good. Getting ready to meet the players to tell them their good news. Tomorrow we start learning plays."

"That's going to be great. By the way I've come up with a few new ones."

"Really? I want to see them. Later, when we get back from the meeting." Oliver wondered when she'd come up with them. They were together most of the time. But he really wanted to take a look; she always came up with the most interesting and original plays imaginable.

"Sounds great," she said.

Maxine absolutely loved her life at this moment in time. She couldn't imagine how it could get any better. She was very much in love with what she firmly believed was the man of her life, and the time they spent together devising plays and seeing them executed on the field was thrilling. It certainly was better than military strategies where the goal was war and conquering the enemy. Football without a doubt had brilliant tactics but there were no devastating casualties other than losing a game and disappointing fans, and sometimes unfortunate injuries. It was a give and take in every way.

Oliver and Maxine arrived at the training facility and met up with the rest of the staff and the hopeful players. The coach motioned for all of them to take a seat. He looked at each of the young men in front of him. He was sure they were nervous and their blood pressure slightly elevated by the anticipation of how making the team, or not, would change their lives.

Oliver never liked giving the hopeful players negative results, but today was different as all the players made the cut even though not too many had come to tryout. They were all good players, a couple of them had great potential and the unconventional international athletes would be part of the team as well. He knew they would be extra effort as they hadn't grown up with American football. They were raw when it came to the sport, but superb in their particular athletic field. With hard work, fine-tuning and some imagination Oliver was confident they would become a proper team. He knew the original players who were now laid up had brought their hearts to practices and the games. He was also sure the newest recruits would be just as eager and willing. And that was half the battle.

Oliver was ready for the announcement, as were the men looking at him. They collectively held their breath and when their new coach told them they were part of the team they exhaled and shouted with joy—their lives had just changed—they were the newest members of a professional football team. They were New Mexico Natives.

"You have to understand that the upcoming game, which is only ten days away, can only be won with one thing," Oliver said. "Yes, you have talent, strength and speed, and we need all of that. But that is not enough. The way you'll beat the other team is with heart and brains. You need to think, and quickly, while you're on the field."

"And execute the plays flawlessly," George added.

"Also, I don't want to lose ANY yards because of penalties, not to mention the effort you put in to get those yards. No false starts, no helmet collisions, and absolutely no personal fouls like punching the other guy. Not only is it useless and kills your focus of the game, but you are an example to every youngster watching. You are professional football players and they look up to you, not only because of your talent, but because of your character as well. Understood?" This was very dear to Oliver's heart. Football for some was just a game, but for this man it was also a way to help youngsters. If children were busy with sports and other activities such as music and art, they tended to be engrossed in a passion that would keep them focused and most importantly away from negative influences such as drugs.

"Yes, Coach!" They shouted.

"We don't have the time to learn too many plays, but the ones we do we must know inside and out and in our sleep." Oliver looked at his players and said: "Please dream about them," he chuckled.

"Yes, Coach! They answered.

"Take the rest of the day off because tomorrow morning we start, and it will be harder than you ever imagined. Because we are toward the end of the season and haven't been together as a team we will have to work longer hours, condition harder and practice plays over and over. You will probably want to give up, which I hope you won't. You might vomit from the physical exhaustion, and you will possibly hate my guts for putting you through hell. But I think you will forgive me when we have great results and win our games. If you think you can't handle any of this you are free to go and no one will fault you." Oliver looked at the men. "Any takers?" No one moved. "Very well then, let this be a new beginning for all of us."

They all knew Oliver would keep his pledge. The players as well would give him and the coaches their all. "Yes, Coach!"

"Now, get out of here. We'll see you tomorrow morning."

"Yes, Coach!"

Oliver and Maxine went back to the apartment. She showed him the plays she had envisioned the night before. As always she amazed him.

"These are really good, Max."

"You think so?"

"Absolutely. We'll definitely use them."

CHAPTER 23 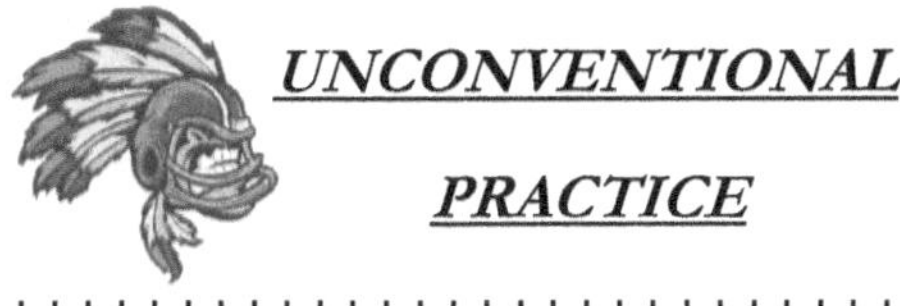 UNCONVENTIONAL PRACTICE

The next morning the players headed out of their apartments and down to the lobby at the scheduled time. The bus arrived a few minutes later. They boarded and headed for their first practice, whether they were new players or part of the original team who had lost so many of their teammates. There was an excitement in the air, one that was new and alluring, an enthusiastic exhilaration that many had only dreamed about but were now a part of. At their destination they headed for the locker room.

Oliver, George, Maxine, and other assistants were already there waiting for them. The players filed in and waited for the heads of the team to talk to them.

Oliver only had a few words for them: "As I said yesterday I want you to use your brains. I want you to use not only your skills but your head as well, otherwise we won't get very far. Pay attention to what your coaches are telling you and remember the details of the plays. Okay, that's all for now. Get your gear on and let's get out there."

"Yes, Coach," the players said.

True to his word Oliver put them through a grueling workout. He started with the warmup which including stretching and jumping rope for quite a long time. He wanted the players to become as light as possible and also strengthen their ankles. The pounding they took on the field was brutal and he wanted to avoid injuries as much as possible. Ahiga in particular was having a difficult time with the rope as it was a little short. It was tough for the triplets as well because their bodies were not meant to be light but heavy. It was the main prerequisite in the sumo ring. Zorba, Delmar, Bart and Jacques on the other hand were rather enjoying themselves as did most of the lighter team members. When they were finished with their rope workout Maxine took over with her own Aikido exercises. The original players chuckled as they remembered their first encounter with the black belt and knew what the new players were in for. "*Endaxi Stratigina,* okay, General," Zorba said to Maxine in Greek. Little did the man know that the woman was an expert in military strategy.

Oliver and George had been watching Delmar and Zorba. Once the two men finished their warmups they included a couple of additional exercises of their own. Delmar did extra stretches for his legs, a sprinter and hurdler's exercises to strengthen and loosen specific muscles for that discipline. Zorba did additional stretches attributed to gymnastics. Of course he also practiced some footwork which he did with lightning speed. Oliver and George liked what they saw, turned to each other and grinned. They knew if a player needed to 'hurdle' an opponent their muscles would have be toned and the muscle memory would probably give them the advantage needed. And Zorba's fast footwork would definitely help in many ways.

The players were still pretty much lined-up when Oliver called them. Once he had everyone's attention, he announced that they would be adding Zorba's and Delmar's exercises. He asked the two men to show the other players what they did.

The players watched, groaning at the idea of having to do more exercises, but they were young enough to understand that their coaches were teachers and they followed their directions as they knew it was for their betterment. The big guys' faces sported a child-like wonder mixed with some degree of apprehension. Oliver noticed and told them they didn't have to do any of the Zorba exercises such as bridges but should try the footwork. He did want them to do Delmar's stretches, though.

The players did rather well, but when some of the big guys like the triplets tried the footwork, they literally fell over their own feet and went down hard.

"No, no, look at me," Zorba said, trying to show them again. "I will show you a dance step called *tsalimaki*. It is the main step in the syrtaki dance. Everybody ready?

What could they say? "Ready!"

"Good. Now stand on your left leg. With your right toe kick the heel of your left foot, then bring it up in front like your kicking a ball slowly and then bring it back and cross it in front of your left leg. Then bring it back and next to your left foot and stop. That is *tsalimaki*."

They followed Zorba's direction and tried it, but by now it was more of a comedy of errors. Instead of getting frustrating there was more laughter than anyone could have thought possible at a football practice.

"I like their mood," Maxine said to Oliver and George.

"Nothing like laughter. It's good for them," George said.

"Yes, it's bringing everyone closer while strengthening them," Oliver agreed.

The coaches and their assistants split up. They had met before the players arrived and now they were each on a mission. Due to the accident and players no longer available for the original positions they had to rearrange plays and strategies. They strategically came up with who would play what position, or positions, if players were needed to double up.

Oliver went off with Ahiga and Neil. The big man would be the new center and he and the quarterback had to know each other almost as well as a couple. They did, however, have an advantage. They had spent time together in the sweat lodge and on the drives back and forth to it. The two men liked each other and would work well together. Oliver spoke with them and told them what to work on. He wasn't worried about those two. They just needed to practice, especially the details and communications between center and quarterback.

Oliver continued with Jacques. The Frenchman would be more of a problem. He wasn't a natural in American football and his instincts stemmed from rugby. Oliver had to realign the European man's mind so that his automatic moves would be molded to the American sport. He explained parts of a play to Jacques and to other players standing in front of him. When Oliver thought they were ready they tried it out. The backup quarterback passed it to Jacques who caught it and started to run but when one of the linebackers came at him Jacques threw it behind him. Of course the player a few feet behind never expected the ball and wasn't able to catch it. Oliver closed his eyes, but the man had patience—for the moment. He went to the rugby player and reminded him that this was American football and they went over the play again.

They tried it a second time. It was better. On the next try, however, Jacques and Zorba were running when the quarterback threw the ball in their direction. Jacques knew he wouldn't be able to catch it and saw that Zorba needed to be either taller or farther down the field. Jacques did what he thought best. He would do a lineout lift, a unique rugby move, one that is usually executed by two players. Jacques figured that Zorba didn't weigh that much. As the little Greek jumped up to catch the ball Jacques grabbed the smaller player's thighs and lifted him up to where Zorba's feet were at the height of the Frenchman's chest. Zorba wasn't that well versed in this kind of football and thought this was a great move. He easily caught the ball. Jacques let go of his legs and Zorba took off. Everyone on the field stood watching with their mouths open. *What the hell was that?*

Maxine went up to Oliver and smiled.

"Did you see that?" He asked.

"Uh, huh, it's called a lineout and it's done by two guys. Jacques is pretty amazing to do that by himself."

"But that's not done in football. Can you imagine what kind of penalty we would get?" Oliver stated, exasperated.

"Fifteen yards?"

"Correct!"

"We'll just have to tell him that it's an illegal move."

"You think?"

"But it was pretty, though, wasn't it?"

"Yeah," Oliver agreed, grumbling. Then he smiled and said: "Imagine if we did use it. We'd blow everybody's mind!"

"Yes, darling, we would."

"Anyway, let me go tell Jacques that the lineout thing is a no-no."

Jacques' saving grace was that he was built strong, really strong, so that when he went barreling through the opponent's defense the man seemed to swallow the earth to get farther down toward his destination. He was tough to stop and he was quick. He would be crucial to earning the coveted yards the team would need to get a first down or to cross into an end zone.

On the other side of the field George was working with the sumos. He showed the triplets one of his favorite moves. He took two of the brothers, faced them toward each other and put their arms on the other's chest. He then took one of their arms and lifted it in the air and made the other brother move to the side and around. "And that's called a forklift," he said. "Got it?"

They practiced a couple of times. As Oliver had predicted they were fast learners. "Got it, Coach," the triplets said.

"You three are going to be on offense. You will be both sides of the center and guarding the QB. I don't want any player from the opposing team to get through you. You have to hold them off."

The Samoans nodded back.

Oliver and George positioned the players the way they thought would work best: Ahiga was the center, the triplets were guards and a tackle. Toma was on the right, Ualesi and Viliamu on the left. Behind Ahiga was Neil, the quarterback. They placed Jacques in the fullback position behind Neil and Zorba as a tailback. They believed Bart would be great as a wide receiver and they decided to try Delmar as a wide receiver as well on the other end. They were still worried about the Jamaican's butter fingers and would have to build the play around that unfortunate detail.

Oliver and George explained their next play: Zorba would receive the ball from Neil and would head down the field. They wanted to see how far he could get, and hopefully wouldn't be crushed too badly. The players did as directed. When Zorba was ready to get crumpled by the defense, he held the ball tight, put his other hand on the ground, pushed hard into a round-off and followed it with a high back tuck over the linebacker in front of him. They all watched as he sailed over the big man, landed on his feet and sprinted into the end zone. He ended with his usual 'Zorba dance stance'.

"What was that?" George asked.

"I think that was part gymnastics, part football," Oliver answered.

"A one handed cartwheel into a backward somersault," Maxine added and then asked: "But it was legal, right?"

The two men looked at her and answered together: "Uh, huh."

"Maybe we should call that a 'Mykonos'?" Maxine volunteered.

"Wasn't a play," George answered.

"Right."

The next play they ran was similar. Zorba was tiny enough to squeeze through the linebackers legs and time and time again the man had the amazing ability to avoid getting crushed by massive bodies. The coaches all agreed that Zorba was the most rubbery player they had ever worked with and were incredibly impressed at how he could bypass and sidestep most anything that came at him.

On the next play Oliver had Bart and Delmar next to each other. When all the players were in position Ahiga snapped the ball to Neil. He and the triplets held the defense as if they were a wall. Oliver and George were grinning like Cheshire cats as they realized what kind of weapon they possessed. They knew the other teams would get a tremendous and very unwelcome surprise— perfect, they thought.

Neil held the ball as he shuffled into position. He saw Bart and Delmar and quickly threw it to the man he lovingly thought of as Octopus Man. Oh, how he loved how the Italian could catch any ball he threw, no matter how awkwardly it sometimes arrived in those hands. Bart caught it flawlessly and the two men sprinted down toward the end zone. The defense was practically on top of Bart. Out of his peripheral vision he saw Delmar right behind him where he was supposed to be and quickly tossed it back to him. Delmar caught it at the same time Bart was tackled and thrown to the ground. The sprinter hurdled over them and then really put on the speed. No one could catch him.

"What was that play called?" Maxine asked.

"I think we should call it 'Kingston'," Oliver answered.

"Delmar would be proud. He sure did leave everyone behind."

Jacques, who had been watching, threw up his arms in exasperation. "Why can they do that and I can't?"

They also practiced field goals. Since the kickers and punters were laid up Bart was the only one the coaches had any faith in. He was just as good with his feet as he was with his hands.

The players lined up and Ahiga snapped it to Bart for a field goal, but he didn't move. Suddenly a couple of linebackers crushed him to the ground. Bart looked up at the sky and moaned. *Porca miseria*, he grumbled, that hurt!

Oliver rushed over to Bart: "You can't take your time! You're not in front of your goal post where both teams are waiting for *you*. This isn't soccer—these guys want that ball and they're going to come at you fast. Understand?"

"*Sì, sì*, okay!"

Oliver gave him his hand and helped him up. "You good?"

"Of course!"

Bart was a quick learner. He also didn't like getting hit by guys made of cement. The next time the ball was snapped to him he caught it and immediately kicked it. No delays. Just pure perfection into where it needed to sail. And he could do it every time.

The coaches and players continued their practice and doubled some of the players into some positions on special teams. One of them was Bart and George explained exactly what was needed.

Bart practiced what he was told and once he understood more of the rules and regulations he had an idea. He went off to one side of the field and tried some kicks. When he was satisfied he went up to Oliver, George and Maxine. "*Vieni qua*, come, I show you something special you will need to win games," Bart said excitedly. He had lined up several balls in kicking tees. He looked at the trio watching. "Are you ready?" They nodded. Zorba was one of the players lined up on the kicking team. Bart took a few steps back behind the position where the ball was set up. "Ready?" He repeated.

"Ready," they answered, wondering what the Italian was up to.

Bart took a last look at the field around him and made a mental note of the twenty yards distance between the ball and the player in front of him. He raised himself on his toes, took a couple of steps and kicked the ball hard, low, yet straight so as not to hit the ground. It shot forth with such speed that it hit the opposing player right below the knee. To everyone's surprise and amazement the ball bounced back to the kicker's line and landed in

Zorba's hands. The little man took off running toward his zone and then stopped.

"You like?" Bart asked his coaches.

"Sure, that was great," George said, "and a fluke," he mumbled inaudibly.

"What are you trying to do exactly?" Oliver asked

"I kick the ball to the enemy but he doesn't know what I am doing. It hits his leg so hard that it returns to one of our players and makes touchdown. I do again, watch."

Oliver, George and Maxine humored him and watched.

The players were back in position and Bart yelled: "Ready?"

"Ready," they answered back.

As with the first kick Bart repeated the same exact play, not with the same player but the one next to him, and again the ball bounced off his leg and came back toward the player next to Bart.

"What the…?" George said.

Oliver looked at Bart. "You can do that every time?"

"Of course, every time," the Italian man answered. And he kicked all the lined-up balls the same way.

"I have never, ever seen anything like it," George said.

"You and me both, and anybody else for that matter," Oliver said, and looked as if he had just witnessed a miracle. He turned to Bart. "Tell me, can all soccer players do such a thing?"

"Oh, no, only the really good ones, like me," he answered grinning.

"But you were a goalkeeper, usually the forwards are the ones with such skills," Maxine said.

"That is true, and I was a forward, but I did not have the stamina required for running constantly. *Per fortuna* I had good hands also.

"*Bravo, Bartolomeo!*" Maxine said.

"*Grazie.*"

"I think we will definitely use this play when we need it. Hey, Bart, how about we call this play *Venice.*"

"Oh, yes, *perfetto*. Is good."

"That sure is a new style of so-called onside kick," George said.

"You said that right. Pretty amazing," Oliver added.

"Uh, huh, sure is."

"And I like the name you gave it," Maxine said.

"Alright, let's call it a day," Oliver said.

"Sounds good," George agreed and told the team to end the practices.

CHAPTER 24

FIRST GAME

AFTER ACCIDENT

The coaches, staff and players were in the locker room almost ready to take the field. For some it would be their first professional game, for others it would be bitter-sweet as their original teammates were no longer with them. Thankfully they had all survived the crash but wouldn't be able to play for quite some time.

Oliver stood in front of the players and said: "Gentlemen, I would like to dedicate this game to our team members who went through a tragic event and can't be with us, although I know they're here in heart and spirit. Let's make our boys proud, gentlemen. This game is for them."

"Yes, Coach!"

"Alright, finish up and let's get out there."

Ahiga spoke up. "Uh, Coach?"

"Yes?"

"Would you mind if I smudged everyone?" The players and the coaches looked at the big man. Neal immediately thought of the sweat lodge. They all wondered what the Indian had in mind. Ahiga quickly continued: "It's no different than incense in a church, or at a Buddhist temple or in a mosque. It is for protection and unity. It is a tradition among the Native Americans to do a ceremony before something important and to cleanse anxieties and unwanted energies away. And we are, after all, the Natives."

"What are you smudging us with?" Delmar asked slyly. Oliver threw him a dirty look. "Just wonderin', Coach," the Jamaican said smiling.

"White sage," Ahiga answered.

"I think it's a wonderful idea and can only help bring good results," Maxine said. The professor had studied rituals as well as many wars which had begun because of religious beliefs, but they also performed ceremonies.

"How long will it take?" Oliver asked.

"Just a couple of minutes," Ahiga replied.

"Guys?" Oliver said looking at the players.

"Hey, we'll take all the help from the Spirits we can get," Neil said, remembering how much Ahiga and the sweat lodge had helped.

The team respected and trusted Neil. He was a good leader and a little sweet smoke could only help to bring everyone together. "Yeah, let's do it," the team hollered.

"Alright, but do it quickly," Oliver said. "Ahiga, what do you want us to do?"

"Everybody gather in a tight circle." They did. "Hold hands and close your eyes. Breath gently and relax." They did that too. "Now, I'm just going to light the sage and pass the smoke over your heads. We'll be done in a couple of minutes."

Ahiga took the bundled leaves, which looked like the biggest reefer Delmar could ever imagine, and lit one of the ends while inwardly praying to the Spirits. The flame represented fire. When the herbs, which symbolized the earth, were smoking he put the wad in a big shell, which in turn represented water. Ahiga took a coveted eagle feather, the symbol for air, and quickly circulated the smoke over himself as he had to be 'clean' before he smudged anyone else. The big man held the shell with the smoke above his teammates and used the feather to scatter the little clouds around each one. He smiled as the waves of gray and white moved differently for each member of the team. Most of them were picturing themselves on the field playing the best football they ever had, whether they were a wide receiver scoring a touchdown or a linebacker diverting a throw by the opposing team's quarterback. Delmar dreamed of Rosalie, the love he left behind on the island in the West Indies. Perhaps it was the smell that triggered the vision.

A couple of minutes later Ahiga was finished. "Okay, everybody, we're done," he announced.

"That's a pity," Delmar said, "but thanks, man."

"Yes, thank you, Ahiga. That really was lovely," Maxine said, and she meant it. A peacefulness had enveloped her when he had smudged her.

Ahiga nodded and smiled. The lady was 'connected', he mused.

They all put a hand in the middle of the circle and shouted: "HONEEZNÁ!"

"Alright, gentlemen," Oliver said. "Let's get out there and show them what we're capable of!"

"Yes, Coach!"

It was the first time the locker room didn't reek of perspiration, instead it smelled of sweet sage. The players left for the field. Ahiga put away the shell and herbs. He quickly took the ashes in his hand and followed his teammates. When he arrived on the field he opened his hand and let the charred residue fall on the grass and fly into the air.

The stadium was filled to capacity. The fans were present, as were VIPs and celebrities. They all wanted to support the Natives, especially because this was the first game after the accident. Not only did they want to watch their team in what they were sure would be another wonderful game, but they were also present to show the players that had been hurt that they were thinking of them.

"He can't be more than 5.5," a woman shrieked from the stands as she noticed Zorba.

"Maybe he's a punter or kicker."

"Naw," another fan said, "I heard he's a receiver or something."

"They're going to break him into little sticks!" the woman moaned again. "Oh, and he's so handsome!"

The men laughed.

Another woman in the stands took out her mascara, did her lashes, dipped the brush back into the container and then smeared the brush above her cheeks making a black design as if a cat had scratched her, without the bleed of course. She looked at the people staring at her. "It's the new version of 'anti-glare'," she explained.

Tony Schuster and Laura Sullivan were back in their booth and started broadcasting the game.

"This is another big day for the Natives," Laura said. "If they win today they're going to the *big* game! That would be amazing!"

"But highly unlikely as they lost so many good players in that horrific accident."

"They had a really good chance, up until two weeks ago when a truck plowed into a minibus carrying a bunch of their players," Laura said. "What happened to the Natives is truly heartbreaking. Thankfully they all survived, but there were a lot of broken bones and a couple of them were on the critical list for a while. Some of the players will be laid up for weeks because of their injuries."

"They're a tough bunch of guys. Hopefully they'll just need time to heal."

"They lost their center and most of their offensive line," Laura said.

"And their kickers and punters. It looked promising for them, although I had my reservations about Neil Howard."

"Yeah, I'm with you, Tony. He did worry me at first, but he looks really good and seems to have gotten his act together."

"You were right. He did come back strong. I'm looking at the new roster and I've never heard of any of these guys. How about you?"

"Nope, me neither, and their public relations guy was pretty vague. Usually Isaac Cohen is very meticulous."

"Yeah, he's one of the best, but I have a feeling he's done it on purpose—kind of a surprise effect maybe. Where did these guys come from?" Tony asked, hoping that Laura with her love of statistics would know some details about the new players. "The majority of them look like they're just out of high school. They're so young! Maybe they still have their baby teeth!"

"The new players are the ones who didn't make the cut in Indiana or their first tryout for the Natives. And some of them are new to football, American football. This is one crazy team," Laura laughed, reading the information on the new players. "There's Bartolomeo Bacci, an Italian who used to be a soccer player."

"Ah, must be their kicker."

"Jacques Dupont, a Frenchman who used to be a rugby player.

"Yeah, I can see that."

Laura continued: "A gymnast who is also a dancer…"

"A dancer? What kind of dancer?"

"Well, Greek dances of course. His name is Zacharias Papa… oh, Christ!"

"What?" Tony asked, wondering what the problem was.

"I can't pronounce that name," Laura wailed, "not to mention that it's a yard long." She took a deep breath. "Okay, I'm going to do this."

"Do what?"

"His last name. Papa… gramma… ti… ko… pou… los. I did it!" She exclaimed excitedly.

"Good on you, but there's no way we're going to be able to say his name during the game," Tony chuckled.

"True. How about we call him Papa-g, or Zorba?"

"Where did you get Zorba?"

"That's his nickname, he's a dancer remember. Maybe they named him after the movie."

"You've seen the movie?" Tony asked.

"Hey, I might be a little young, but I'm a movie buff and Zorba the Greek is a classic."

"That it is, my young friend," Tony chuckled. "I agree we should call him Papa-g or Zorba. Would that be okay with our viewers?" He asked, as if the people watching them on television could answer. "I didn't hear any objections," he joked, "at least not for the moment. So, what do we know about this guy?"

"It's his first pro football game. He used to be quite the college gymnast," Laura answered.

"Which explains his height and weight. He can't be more than a hundred and sixty pounds soaking wet. He sure doesn't fit the ideal football physique."

"He's going to get creamed out there," Laura said. "At 5'5" he's one of the shortest players ever." "Ha, look at his name on his jersey. There are so many letters you can hardly read it."

"They should have just put Zorba on it. That would have been an easy solution, for all of us."

"I agree. This should be interesting. Any other beauties?"

"Oh, yes. There's a Jamaican sprinter who got bounced off his Olympic team because of 'special' cigarettes."

"Special *Jamaican* cigarettes?" Tony chuckled.

"Uh, huh."

"And I'm sure all the tests he's taken are squeaky clean, otherwise he wouldn't be able to play."

"That's affirmative. He was born here and has no record with the police. He went back to Montego Bay as a kid where his parents were from. When he was older he had a little something going on with the daughter of the chief of police and he wound up in Albuquerque."

"Oh, I see, don't mess with daddy's little girl," he laughed.

"Exactly."

"Who else is new on the team?"

"Well, you know how we sometimes analyze triplets?"

"Quarterbacks, running backs and wide receivers, or on the defense, linemen, backside linebackers and defensive backs?"

"Yeah," Laura answered. "Well, now we've got *real* triplets."

"As in brothers?"

"Yep. Identical ones too. "You're going to love this one… Samoan triplets, formerly sumo wrestlers. They're six feet six inches tall and weigh 360 pounds each."

"Christ, this sounds like a circus!"

"It gets better."

"How?"

"There's a real Native on the team, a Navajo, from one of the Reservations, and he's seven feet tall! His name is Ahiga Yazzi, which by the way means 'he fights'."

"Well, that should work for the Natives. Is this supposed to be their version of Gronkowsky?"

"Maybe, but he's actually a little taller than Gronk."

"And probably not as fast."

"Probably one of the reasons he's a center and not a tight end," Laura agreed.

"Right."

The Natives' special team took the field. When they were lined up, Bart looked up. *"Buongiorno a tutti!"* He shouted, lifted his arms out toward the spectators and bowed to the opposing players and the crowd in the stadium. The refs look at each other. *Was that legal?* Before they could call a penalty, Bart kicked the ball long and it sailed smoothly through the goal posts. It was his first time in an American football game and of course he had to show off, just a little.

The opposing team now had the ball and the players lined up, but there would be no score as the Natives' held back the opposition like a finely oiled machine since thankfully the Natives' defense hadn't lost any players.

The broadcasters watched as the Natives, led by Neil Howard took the field. They marveled at the big Samoans on the line of scrimmage.

"They look like a piece of the great wall of China!" Tony said.

"Yeah, a thousand pound fence!"

One of the men from the opposing team across from Toma, one of the triplets, asked: "What were you guys, ten pound babies?"

"Naw, we were triplets, only nine pounds."

Did he mean each? The opponent wondered, but continued to rib them. "Well, if your Mama had quads instead of triplets you Michelin boys would have been a pickup truck."

"Don't ever say nothin' about our mother," Viliamu hissed.

"No, make that a monster truck," the opposing player continued.

"You should have listened to my brothers," Ualesi said with a conclusive sigh.

The man didn't have time to respond with another crack as Ahiga snapped the ball. Toma grabbed the demeaning player by the side of his pants as if he were wearing a *mawashi*, a sumo's loincloth belt, and pulled hard as he lifted him effortlessly up high and fast. It was a move he had done a thousand times while wrestling. The man yelped and the crowd collectively groaned as if they too could feel the pain of the wedgie pulling the player's testes, probably all the way up to his intestines. When Toma let him go the opposing player dropped down hard. He lay on the grass and one of his teammates held out his hand and helped him up. He mumbled a thank you as he was breathing with some difficulty and his gait was a little uneven. None of the opposing players ever made fun of the triplets again.

"Ouch, that was quite the uncomfortable tightening of the pants," Laura cringed.

"Yeah, but I think that guy felt far worse than just uncomfortable," Tony said, trying not to think of his own genitals.

"And, yes," she said, watching the referee. "He's probably going to call a penalty for 'unnecessary roughness', or maybe it'll be for 'holding by the offense'," she chuckled.

Tony realized the fans were shouting something. "What are they saying?" He asked, wondering why the spectators were yelling.

"T.U.V!" Laura answered.

"I'm not even going to try to guess. What is that?"

The crowd was collectively screaming: "T.U.V! D.F.S!"

"What are they chanting?" Tony asked.

"T.U.V! D.F.S!" Laura answered.

"Yeah, I got that, but what does it mean?"

"It's the Samoans, T.U.V. Toma, Ualesi and Viliamu, their names. And D.F.S. is defense."

"Oh, brother, leave it to the fans to start a new fad." Tony said.

Ahiga snapped the ball perfectly to Neil who stepped back to give his runners a chance to get downfield. The triplets were a solid wall and kept their quarterback safe and gave him the time he needed. Neil did a couple stutter steps and then threw a perfect and beautiful spiral to Bart who caught it and ran for ten yards before he was stopped.

From the fifty-yard line Ahiga snapped the ball again and Neil repeated another amazing throw, this time to Zorba. The little man caught it close to the sidelines on the thirty and sprinted toward the end zone. An edge rusher lunged hard at his legs but it was impossible to stop Zorba's lighting fast feet as he stopped abruptly, jumped up and pulled away. The defenseman flew by him into the group standing on the side where his teammates caught him as he landed into them. Zorba continued running and watched two more opponents coming straight for him.

"Zorba is almost in the end zone, he's on the ten but there are two big guys in his way!" Tony hollered, almost as fast as Zorba was running. "They're coming fast and furious! He doesn't have a chance, they're going to stop the little man and he's going to get hit hard."

"Wait! What is he doing… " Lauren exclaimed, "holy sh… sugar…"

It wasn't often, but both announcers were speechless as they watched Zorba do a front tuck over the two tall defensemen who ran into each other. As they lay dazed on the ground they looked up and over their heads as if they were watching a comic book hero flying by. Zorba landed in the end zone and scored.

"Touchdown!" Laura screamed.

"What was that?" Tony asked.

"I'm pretty sure that was a somersault."

"Was that a play?"

"Uh, the Mary Lou Retton?" Laura replied, lacking a better answer.

The broadcasters and spectators watched as the Greek man shouted 'OPA!' and struck the dancing pose with his arms outstretched. He raised his arms, snapped his fingers and danced a few *syrtaki* steps at lightning fast speed. The spectators loved it.

"He does look like Anthony Quinn in Zorba the Greek," Tony remarked.

They continued watching as the rest of the team ran up to him.

"Hey, boys," Zorba said, "my first touchdown! Let's do a *tsalimaki*! You remember?"

The players nodded. They quickly formed a line, put their arms on each other's shoulders and did the Greek dance step Zorba had shown them during practice. It only took a moment and then they did their Native American trademark dance steps with the mascot next to them.

From the sidelines the coaches and staff were hollering and watching the players in the end zone.

"Ahiga looks a little like a dancing bear," Oliver said.

"Surrounded by his cubs," Maxine chuckled.

George just stood there with his arms crossed over his chest and grinned. Man, did he adore his team.

Up in the broadcasters' booth Tony was smiling as well. "You know, Laura, I love football and it's been my life, but these young Natives have taught me, or should I say reminded me, that it is a game not only love but to enjoy and have fun. Really have fun! It's a seed that was planted in us during childhood. We have loved this sport ever since, but somewhere along its growth it got way too serious. It's of course big business as well and as much as we all love football, from the owners to the fans, it seems we need to be reminded every once in a while why we love the sport—we can't forget the fun of it!"

"Very true, Tony."

The teams were tied with one touchdown apiece. The Natives were in command of the ball and when Neil received the snap he threw it to Bart who was not quite in position. The ball bounced off his shoulder and the Italian felt it land between his shoulder and his neck. Instead of reaching up to grab it he pushed his helmet down hard on the ball and kept it there just long enough to confuse the opposing players who thought the ball had fallen. Where *was* the ball? By the time they saw what was happening Bart was now holding it firmly and flying into the end zone.

"Are you kidding me? What was that neck thing?" Tony screamed.

"He's a soccer player."

"I've never seen anything like it in my life."

"Hey, you're watching the Natives. You never know

what you'll see from them. I would call that a unique touchdown."

Bartolomeo Bacci pumped his fists in the air, acknowledged the crowd and ran enthusiastically onto the field. After a few yards he slid on his knees.

"Oh, no, this isn't soccer!" George cried.

"Tell him that," Oliver said, but couldn't help but chuckle.

"All we need now is a Mexican broadcaster yelling gooooooooaaaaaal!" Maxine laughed.

The Natives were given a penalty. They would have to explain why to Bart. It seemed no one had told him the problem of too much celebrating after a touchdown.

The Natives' opponents scored on their next drive. The team was an old established organization and they were often in the playoffs. They were good, very good, and now one touchdown ahead. The ball reverted back to the Natives.

On the next play Zorba was to Neil's right, crouching low with his head down. Ahiga snapped the ball to Neil who immediately put it in Zorba's hands, but Zorba still didn't move. Neil took several steps back and looked downfield for a receiver and faked a throw. At the same instant Delmar plucked it from Zorba and took off running. The defensive players hadn't noticed Delmar with the ball until he ran past. By the time they rushed after him his lead was too big and he flew into the end zone.

"What was that?" Tony blurted.

"A really cute fake," Laura chuckled, answering his colleague.

"I'll say. And Delmar sure can run! Does he look like a cheetah when he's running or what?"

"I agree. Speed, elegance and athleticism—the fastest cat on earth."

"With dreadlocks."

"Right."

Delmar could hardly stop himself after he ran into the end zone. He kept going until he hit the pads on the wall below the bleachers. A woman screamed from the stands: DELMAR, BABY, WILL YOU MARRY ME?

Delmar looked up into the stands to where the voice came from. He saw the woman, and the fans, waiting for his answer, grins on their faces from ear to ear. Delmar hollered back to the woman: "ARE YOU RICH, MY PRETTY?"

The crowd roared with laughter and clapped. Delmar kissed the ball, threw it into the crowd toward the woman, waved and took off. Several people tried to catch it. The man closest to the flirty woman caught the ball and offered it to her. "I'm single," he said.

"What'cha doin' after the game, handsome?" She asked.

The spectators laughed and clapped again. They were having a good time, not just with the Natives and the game but with their fellow aficionados.

The teams were tied again. The Natives were in possession of the ball and the clock was running down to just over one minute. If they lost this would be some of the players' only game and their season would be over. If they won, they would be the division champs and headed to the biggest game of the year.

The entire stadium was on its feet. The drums were resounding incessantly. The fans were either screaming, chanting or holding their breath. Thousands of people in the stadium, and millions watching on televisions, were focused on the next few seconds of the most unforeseeable outcome from the most unconventional plays and players.

At the fifty-yard line the Natives listened to Neil.

"Ten, twenty-three, Istanbul!" The quarterback hollered.

The opponents wondered what the hell this city was about. They had already heard 'Oxford', 'New York' and 'Kingston'. They were about to find out. Ahiga snapped the ball to Neil who gave it to Jacques. Delmar and Bart were right behind him. The three men took off. Jacques ran down the sideline until a safety started tackling him. Before he went down he passed the ball behind him to Delmar. That was why it was called Istanbul, because the city was on two continents and the play was for two players. But Delmar dropped it.

The entire stadium groaned.

"Mister Butter Fingers," George mumbled.

Oliver immediately called a time out. Fifty seconds left on the clock. The coach knew they would go into overtime if they didn't score and he knew his young team wasn't up for it. They surely had the stamina as they had been well trained, but they hadn't had enough of it and they certainly didn't have the experience of overtime quarters, especially the new players.

They were back on the fifty-yard line, on their second down.

Throughout the game Jacques had been indispensable. He always managed to get the extra yards or even inches the team needed. It seemed the Frenchman was made of bricks. Opposing players bounced off him and Jacques barreled through as if he were a battering ram. The Natives were going for the win with less than a minute left on the clock. In the huddle Neil gave the players an extra two plays. The Natives lined up. Neil received the snap and immediately handed the ball to Jacques. The sumos held the defensemen and suddenly two of them pushed harder and opened a hole for the Frenchman. He slid through, twirled himself away from a couple more opponents and made enough progress to get five yards before getting tackled. Neil immediately had his line in position, much to the dismay of the other team. The Natives remembered the instructions from the huddle. There were now forty seconds left on the clock.

Neil handed the ball again to Jacques who barreled through several players until he was pinned down before he could get any further. He also couldn't get to the side of the field so the clock wasn't stopping. Oliver asked for a timeout, their last one.

"Did he get to the Natives' thirty-five?" Laura asked.

"It looks like it, but I'm not sure."

Had they gotten those crucial ten yards? The opponents' coach didn't think so and he couldn't afford a field goal from the Natives that would lose them the game. He called for a challenge.

"Yup, there it is, he threw out his red flag," Tony said.

The chain gang brought out the rods. The stadium was almost silent as they watched one of them position one of the sticks on the forty-five-yard marker. Everyone looked at the field and on the jumbotron. The second member of the crew pulled the ten-yard chain until it was taunt. The ball was short by less than an inch. A collective groan came from the spectators. The Natives felt the same way. Their opponents, however, were thrilled.

They lined up just short of the thirty-five with twenty seconds on the clock.

"T.U.V! D.F.S! " The crowd screamed. "T.U.V! D.F.S!" they insisted.

After the snap Ahiga planted his feet hard and stood with his legs apart. He was as rigid as a marble statue. The triplets on either side of him moved forward and in front of their center. They did it so quickly that they were just a tan and dark amber blur. It was just enough for Neil to dive through Ahiga's legs and get the coveted inches they needed to continue their drive.

"T.U.V! T.U.V!" the spectators loved their Samoan sumo triplets.

"Well, that was a very smooth quarterback sneak," Tony said.

"Yes, and the crowd seemed very happy with it too," Laura added. "The Natives have their first down."

"But they don't have much left on the clock. I think they'll probably go for a field goal."

"Let's see what Hadley decides. I think he's going to have Kisses kick for the three points," Laura ventured.

"Kisses?"

"That's what his name means—bacci, kisses."

"Well, I'm sure he'll get quite a few if he makes it."

"He's a soccer player, how could he not score?" Laura asked.

Tony was thinking about the double meaning but didn't say anything. He would leave that up to their home viewers.

Bart had not been in the last play. He had been on the sidelines with George who was explaining what he needed from him. Bart understood and prayed to all his saints, especially the Italian ones, that he wouldn't let anyone down.

Every player was in position. Every spectator was standing. It was time. They collectively held their breaths. Bart crossed himself, ran several steps and kicked the oblong sphere from the thirty-five-yard line. The crowd held their breath. Would it fly where it was supposed to? Would the Natives win the game? They watched anxiously as the football flawlessly and perfectly sailed between the yellow goal posts. Bartolomeo Bacci did not let anyone down. He added the three coveted points to win the game and the division. The New Mexico Natives were going to the big game.

The stadium erupted into screams of delight as the drummers pounded the skins harder than they ever had. The fans were so ecstatic and loud that the entire city probably heard them. The players and staff ran onto the field, whooping and hollering with excitement. They had done it! Suddenly the grass was covered with more people than it had ever seen at one time, which included a multitude of cameras and reporters.

When they were finished with interviews and cheers from the spectators, the New Mexico Natives headed for the locker room. Before entering the tunnel one of the losing team's fans shouted to Maxine: "Hey, lady, shouldn't you be home cooking dinner?" The crass spectator hollered from the stands.

"Don't fuck with her, asshole, she's got a black belt in Aikido," one of the Native's players walking close to Maxine said.

"In what was that? Kiddos?" The man cackled.

"Nothing but an inconsequential, silly, ignoramus peasant," Maxine said evenly to the player. "No worries, and thanks."

"My pleasure, Lady Max."

"Did he get to you?" Oliver chuckled, having overheard the dialogue.

Maxine looked at him. "Who? The crass, crude cretin?" She was perturbed and angry, but when she saw Oliver laughing and how funny the scene had really been she smiled and said: "I guess the high class snob in me just came out."

"A true aristocrat is not a snob."

"Well said, Oli."

"My pleasure."

"You know what?"

"What?"

"Absolutely nothing can bother me at this moment. If anything we should be celebrating... and I can think of quite a few ways."

"I'll gladly participate in any or even all of your ideas," Oliver answered. Man, he loved everything about her. And he and his team were Division champs and going to the big game! Life could not be more perfect.

CHAPTER 25  THE SEASON'S BIGGEST GAME

Isaac was in heaven. He was one of the best public relations guys in the business, but never in his wildest dreams could he have devised a campaign to promote and elevate this new team so perfectly. He had help from the Natives themselves as they managed, from their own results and their followers, to become the darlings of the League. And for several reasons: They were not only the new kids on the block but also the comeback kids from a devastating loss of players due to the horrific accident. Their fans loved them, the players were movie-star handsome, which elevated the female viewership even more, and they brought unorthodox plays with amazing results. This new, young team had achieved what everyone would have thought impossible and totally ridiculous. They would be the stars in the upcoming game, the biggest and most coveted one of the year. Isaac was part of the group who stood in the locker room directly in front of the players. The excitement was palpable.

Oliver stood in front of his staff and other coaches and faced the players. "Gentlemen, we have achieved the improbable and what everyone thought, the impossible. We have exceeded everyone's expectations, maybe even our own," he chuckled. "I'm proud to be in the presence of such wonderful men and talented players.

"Don't forget most handsome," Maxine chimed in.

"Thankfully we have Lady Max to remind us of the important details."

Everyone laughed, but they knew what an asset Maxine had been to their success. They admired and respected her and loved her like a sister. If she wasn't attached to Oliver they might have perceived her differently. Maxine felt the same way about 'her boys' and as protective as a mother hen, even though they were some of the best-looking specimens fans would gladly throw themselves at.

Oliver continued: "This is the biggest game in football, the one children dream about their whole lives, the one game they not only want to be a part of, but the one they want to win. And it's the fans' game too—the people who have supported you through every game, every play and every kind of foul weather. They can't be on the field but you carry a piece of them with you. You are, we all are, these grown children. Today, this is *our* game." Oliver looked directly at Delmar. "This is our Olympics." The Jamaican nodded his thanks. "It is also our first and will be the most memorable. On this day we write history, not just in the annals of football, but in our own personal ones."

Oliver took a deep breath and looked at his team. "I'm very proud of what we have all accomplished. No one has ever done what we have. I want you to know that no matter if we win or lose this game, in my playbook we have already won. We have given our blood, sweat, tears and our hearts." Oliver stopped. "After today things won't be the same. Some of us might still be together, and I hope so. Others may move on to different endeavors, but on this day, this is who and what we are and have become. I want to thank you, not just for the effort and the soul you have put into this season, but for allowing me into you hearts and permitting me to call you family. I love each and every one of you as if you were my own child for that is how I see you, well maybe not George, but I love him too." They laughed good-heartedly. "You are and will always be a smile in my heart until the end of my days. Thank you for permitting me to be your coach."

"Thank you, coach!" they shouted.

"Oh, and before taking the field Ahiga will do his sage thing. It seemed to help out last time."

"He means the smudging," Maxine volunteered.

"Right. That's it," Oliver concluded.

Ahiga performed his ritual and the players took it very seriously. When he finished Oliver looked at the faces watching him and smiled. He had one last comment for the team: "Now, let's continue making history—let's win!"

The big Navajo man waited until all the players left the locker room and then followed them out. As he had in the previous game the big man inconspicuously dropped the sage ashes from his hand onto the playing field.

Tony and Laura were in the booth already broadcasting, just as excited as everyone else.

"It's thanks to amazing talent and great plays by Hadley that the Natives are here today," Tony said.

"And Lady Maxine had a hand in those plays," Laura added proudly. She had come to greatly respect the English woman.

"It does take a village. These guys were the biggest underdogs ever! Nobody believed they would be in this position and at this event."

"And everyone loves an underdog. Even fans from across the country who don't have a team playing are rooting for the Natives," Laura said. "Their story is incredible and their achievement is unheard of. They've become the darlings of the nation."

"I've never seen so much media. This game gets an average of over one hundred million viewers. From what I hear there are more than a hundred and ten and possibly more. It's even being watched by people who don't really follow football!"

"That's pretty amazing."

"My daughter is watching with a whole group of her friends. They've been planning this for days and she's asked more questions about football in the last couple of weeks than she has in her entire life!"

Laura laughed. "I can see that. The Natives are young, talented and fun. They're creative as well as entertaining, and let's not forget they're a bunch of really good-looking guys."

"They're quite the mix."

"Right. That spices it up as well. And I heard that other countries around the world are watching too."

"You mean besides Canada and Mexico?" Tony asked.

"Oh, yes. The U.K., Italy and Germany usually follow as they have some teams that play American football, but I received a report that France, Greece and Jamaica are following as well. They probably won't know too much about American football but they'll definitely know when the teams score. It's probably thanks to the new international players."

"That's great. More worldwide exposure." Tony watched the tunnel beside the field. "Okay, here we go. The players are coming out," he announced.

Once the opening ceremonies were finished the players took the field. Fans in the stadium and in front of televisions, as well as players from all corners of the nation had anticipated this moment all season long. The stands were filled with jerseys from both teams. It was divided pretty evenly as the event was not being held in either Albuquerque or the opponents' home stadium. The Natives drumming group was present and they beat the skins incessantly. It fueled the passion of the spectators even more.

It was time. The coin toss dictated who would receive the ball first. It was the opposing team. The Natives' special team lined up. Bart crossed himself as he jogged into position and started to raise his arms to wave to the fans and then remembered he couldn't really do that. The referee took a quick look around the field, didn't see anything out of place and blew his whistle. The game was live. The millions of fans reacted with the enthusiasm of a long-awaited event. They screamed and hollered, cheered for the team they loved whether they had been a fan the entire season or just for this particular game. It was also the signal Bart was waiting for. As soon as he heard the whistle he raised his hand and ran toward the football on the tee. His team followed and Bart kicked the ball deep in front of the pylon. As it landed it twisted off the field. The Natives were going to make this game as difficult as possible for their rivals. Their opponents would start on the thirty-five-yard line. George smiled as he remembered Bart's first encounter with an oblong ball.

The Natives' rivals scored during their first outing. They were a strong team that had been in big games before and had won a couple of times. They wanted to do it again.

By the time the game was in the second quarter the score was still 7-0. The Natives' defense was doing a good job but so were their opponents. Up until halftime no one scored any additional points.

The Natives received the ball at the start of the third quarter. They still didn't get very far. On the third down they lined up once again on the line of scrimmage on the rival's thirty-yard line. Ahiga snapped the ball to Neil and the opposing player in front of the big man slipped and fell between the big man's legs. Ahiga quickly squeezed them together and held the player there. He always protected his quarterback, any way he could.

"Did you see that?" Tony said laughing.

"I did. That's a move that I don't think I've seen before."

"I don't think it was planned."

Neil took the snap and dropped back to hand the ball to his tight end Jacques, but quickly pulled the ball back from the hand off, trying to hide it from the defense. He looked downfield for an open receiver. Jacques continued running as if he had the ball. Zorba was running next to him but he suddenly stopped and turned to face Neil who had adroitly just thrown the ball. It landed on Zorba's chest and he clutched it tight and took off running toward the end zone.

"Paga-G, Zorba's got the ball!" Tony hollered.

"And two massive linebackers on his heels," Laura added heatedly.

Zorba could feel the big men closing in on him and then he felt their fingers closing in on his legs and feet but he was so flexible and his foot reflexes so quick that he managed to elude them.

"He's on the ten, on the five!" Tony hollered.

Zorba ran faster than he ever had in his life and one

foot short of the end zone he dove for a touchdown. When he hit the grass he rolled, immediately jumped up and held the ball high over his head. He threw it into the crowd, much to their delight.

"He did it! Touchdown Natives!" Tony shouted again.

Zorba did a standing back tuck and assumed his signature dance pose. The crowd went wild and hollered. His teammates ran up to him and congratulated the man.

"Hey, Zorba, shouldn't we do the *maki* thing, man?" One of the players asked.

"*Tsalimaki*, yes, yes!"

Members of the team lined up quickly and together they did the Greek dance step Zorba had shown them. Their audience loved it. They continued with their Native American steps as was their custom.

The score was now 7-6 and Bart had no problem with the extra point.

"Well, they're even at seven points each," Tony said.

"Let's see what these teams do next," Laura added.

It didn't take long for the opposition to score and they added the extra point by one of their oldest veteran punters, reminiscent of Vinatieri. The score grew to 14-7.

Just before the clock ran down at the end of the third quarter Oliver called a time out and spoke to Neil and the players. He wanted to rattle the opposition a little. The players were huddled around their coach. "Alright, guys, listen up. We're going to play with their minds little."

"It's the Natives' fourth down and they're struggling to get down the field," Tony said.

"They only have thirty seconds before the end of the quarter and they're on the fifty-yard line."

"Hadley just called for a time out. The man is sharp. Let's see what he's got up his sleeve."

The players listened attentively. "Ahiga will snap the

ball on the second 'hut', but Neil I want you to make it long like 'huuuuuuuuuuuuuuut'. I want the other team to false start. Got that everybody?"

"Yes, Coach!"

The players took the field and Neil and the players did exactly what Oliver said. It happened. The opposing team lost five yards.

The Natives did it again and gained another five yards.

"What is wrong with the defense?" Laura asked.

"They keep false starting."

"I know, they've just lost ten yards."

Neil listened to Oliver through the headset.

"Neil, do it again," Oliver said through his mic. Neil lifted his eyebrows. Could they do a third time? As if reading his mind the coach answered the question. "Yes. Do the same thing, normal hut, second long hut. By now their defense knows, but this time add a third very quick hut and snap it on the third. Got it?"

Neil nodded and smiled. He definitely got it. Coach knew what he was doing and he told the other players in the huddle. Some of them chuckled.

The players lined up. They were ready.

Neil called: "Ten, twenty-three, Pamplona, hut, huuuuuuuuuuuuuuut"—one of the rival players moved moved—"HUT!" It happened again and their opponents were certainly rattled. The Natives had just won an easy fifteen yards and lined up on their opponents' own fifteen. On the sideline the other team's coach was cussing up a storm and screaming at his players. He looked like he was ready to slap each one of them. On the next snap Neil knew he would have an extra sliver of time before the defense came at him as they didn't dare lose another five yards. The quarterback quickly handed it off to Jacques who squeezed himself between the

Samoans and barreled into the end zone to score a touchdown.

It had gone as planned. They had executed the 'running of the bull', the 'Pamplona', perfectly.

As with the previous touchdown Bart had no problem with the extra point and the score was tied at 14-14.

At the beginning of the fourth quarter the opposition again wasted no time and were able to score another touchdown and the extra point, giving them a 21-14 advantage. The Natives were now behind and running out of time. However, they were not going to give up. They wanted to be the champs. They had fought hard, overcome obstacles and believed in their souls they were deserving. They would give everything they could to make this a reality.

The time was running down fast and the Natives hadn't progressed. It was also time to kick the ball to their opponents. There were six minutes left on the clock.

As the Natives' special team was ready to take the field George stopped them. "Gentlemen, Bart will do a Venice. Stay sharp. We need the ball back."

"Yes, Coach."

Oliver turned to the Italian goalie. "Any problem, Bart?"

"No, no, *tutto bene*, all good. I make *Venezia perfetto*," he said and ran onto the field. When the players were getting in position Bart placed the football in the tee and adjusted the angle to where he wanted it. Was it his physics or his soccer mind making the adjustment? Maybe a combination of both. In any event when both teams were ready and Bart received the signal to start he kicked the ball hard and straight. It hit a blocker from the return team just below the knee so hard that the player buckled, more in surprise that any real pain. He didn't react fast enough, but couldn't really have caught the ball as it bounced back into the hands of Delmar who had been strategically placed in a tackler position. The Jamaican caught the ball, much to the elation of his coaches and teammates, cradled it tight and took off toward the end zone. He ran as fast as he ever had and for as many yards as possible. The rival team was surprised and tried to stop the runner but the Natives players, who had anticipated the 'Venice' were blocking and clearing a path all around Delmar. Their opponents were right behind them but no one could catch the Olympian. Once he was a couple of steps ahead of the crowd the field was clear and he smoothly scored a touchdown.

"What was that?" Tony asked.

"Do you mean the elegant gazelle or the unusually lucky kick?" Lauran ventured. "Special team plays can completely change a game," Laura said.

"Ya think? Please tell me that was a fluke," Tony exclaimed.

"Delmar isn't usually on special teams, so I couldn't say for sure."

The 'Venice' had been executed perfectly, exactly as in practice when Bart had first shown the coaches.

"I'm changing 'Venice' to 'Aviano'," Oliver said.

"The air force base in Italy near Venice?"

"That's right," Oliver said imitating Bart's Italian accent, "Bartolomeo was *perfetto* indeed and his kick was like a fighter plane."

"Ah, now the air base makes sense." Maxine discovered a side to Oliver she didn't yet know. It included a sense of humor. "Aviano sounds good to me," she laughed.

The score was once again tied at 21-21.

The opposing team tried to score another touchdown

but they failed. They did, however, get a field goal and the numbers changed back in their favor at 24-21. The Natives were trailing by three points and were on the field trying to get another touchdown. Ahiga snapped the ball to Neil but the team was repeatedly unable to score. After the last down Bart was on the twenty-yard line ready to kick for a field goal. With less than twenty seconds on the clock this was do or die. The center snapped the ball to the holder. Bart took his steps and kicked the ball toward the uprights when the nose tackle lunged and was able to block the football with his chest. The ball bounced off him crazily and sailed above and behind Bart's head. The Italian followed the ball with his eyes and his body. The physics professor and professional athlete were furiously calculating and searching for a solution. Bart knew the predicament they were in and he knew he had to do something. The spectators, staff and players all watched in horror. Was this the end of the game? Regardless the Natives didn't have any more downs and certainly wouldn't be able to get enough yards for a first. In any event too many opposing players would bring him down. Bart knew he would be flat on his face in one second, two if he was lucky. He could smell the players behind him. In the next split-second Bart's universe came together, and his body did what his mind was telling him to do. With his back to the oncoming players Bart threw his body back, lifted one leg and kicked the ball backwards and behind him in a scissor-like movement. As he fell he watched and held his breath. The ball sailed over all the players, across the crucial yards of the field and toward the opponent's end zone where it was supposed to. The crowd, the players from both teams and the entire staff watched with open mouths, their faces pointed to the sky, their eyes following the ball. It majestically soared through the goal posts. The reaction of what everyone had just witnessed was probably just as great as it had been when Pelé, Brazil's best-known soccer player, had introduced the original bicycle kick so many decades before.

"What was that?" Tony groaned.

"Holy sh…sugar!" Laura exclaimed. "Okay, that's another first. By the way, Tony, do you have any idea how many times you've said 'what was that?'"

"Hey, it's the Natives, what can I say? Well, the score is tied at twenty-four. It's been an amazing game, one not to be forgotten. The Natives have been extraordinary all season, especially for being a new team in their first foray," Tony said.

"And let's not forget that terrible accident where so many players were laid up."

"You've got to hand it to them. They found new players, and what a bunch! They proved they are here to stay and they are hungry for a win today."

"They certainly are and the win could have gone either way, but their opponents have the ball. It's their second down and they only need fifteen yards with fourteen seconds left. The outcome seems predictable," Laura said.

"Well, miracles do happen. You said that at the first game, remember? Don't give up on the Natives just yet. They've been amazing! And Hadley has shown was a master he is," Tony praised.

"And there it is, he just called his last time out. I wonder what he'll tell his team."

On the side-line the defense was gathered around their head coach. "Gentlemen, we need to hold them with everything you've got. This is the most important play of the season. We can't let them score, we need to go into overtime." The rest of the team quickly huddled together, put their hands on top of each other's and yelled: "HONEEZNÁ!

The Natives defense was ready on the line of scrimmage. Every muscle, every nerve, every cell in their bodies stood at attention. If they were rubber bands they would be stretched to their maximum. The opponents' center snapped the ball to their quarterback who in turn passed it to his tight end who caught it and ran toward the end zone, but one of the Natives' linebackers plowed into him and the ball came loose. It wobbled crazily in the air for a split-second and then dropped fast. When it was just about to the hit the grass, the big defenseman stretched his body as far as he could, almost unnaturally, put his hand palm up on the ground and managed to catch the ball. He quickly scooped it into his chest and held on to it as if he were protecting a baby from certain death. As the opposing team's players piled up over him he thanked Maxine for her Aikido exercises. Never could he have stretched as he had just done without her direction. Although he was on the opponents' ten-yard line, the ball was back in the Natives' hands. They didn't care how far they were from their own end zone; they just knew they were still holding on and hadn't lost the game. On the contrary, even though they had a very limited time they were now in control of the football.

"They've got the ball back!" Tony cried excitedly.

"Yes, that was quite the interception by the defense. Wow, what a stretch for such a big guy!" Laura agreed.

The spectators as well as the Natives went wild. They hollered and screamed—there was hope, even if they were so deep in rival territory!

"Oh, my, maybe this is your miracle, Tony!"

"All they have to do is hold on to the ball for a few

more seconds and then the game will go into overtime."

The clock was stopped at five seconds.

The offense took the field. Oliver told Neil to play it safe. All they had to do was run the clock down. The quarterback nodded and told the men the play. They clapped once and took their positions.

Ahiga handed the ball to Neil who backed up and tried to waste as much time as possible, but one of the cornerbacks on the other team managed to sneak through and was all over him before he could do anything with the ball. He cradled it to his chest but it was punched out so hard that it spun out of control and flew over the cornerback's hand and up above Ahiga. The big, tall man had the presence of mind to reach quickly for it and hold on to it, but he just stood there. He wanted to pass it back to Neil, but his quarterback was still on the ground pinned down, so that wasn't possible. He thought he could just hold it until the time ran out, but he had to move he couldn't just stand there. And then he heard three voices as one. It was coming from the Samoans: "Run for a touchdown," they screamed, "we'll protect you!"

Ahiga did. He headed for the end zone, but it was so damn far! The Sumos surrounded him as closely as they could, their arms and bodies practically interlocked together, forming a human barrier around him.

"The clock is going to run out and I can't imagine the big center going all the way," Tony said.

Some of the spectators held up their D Fence signs, screaming and yelling for their team to keep going. The clock ran down. Ahiga was still running. It was almost a leisurely pace, and the fastest the big man could do, which was fine by the Samoans.

"The ball is firmly in place against his chest, which

seems higher than most players' helmets," Laura laughed, "but can he manage another fifty yards? Surely someone will break down that 'great wall of Samoa'."

One of the defensemen managed to squeeze between two of the triplets and tried to bat the ball out of Ahiga's hands but the big man saw him, held the ball high over his head with one hand and with the other pushed him away as if he were a stuffed toy. The man was instantly on the ground. The spectators were taking in the show, never believing the Natives could still stun them. Many stood with their mouths open and speechless. Others were cheering them on.

Since the run was probably the slowest in history all players from the opposing team were closing in on the biggest Natives, but so did the rest of the New Mexico team, including Jacques, Zorba, Delmar and Neil. They fought hard to squeeze themselves next to the triplets as the Samoans now extended their arms in front and to their sides. The opposing players were bouncing off of them. Delmar lunged at a one of the safeties, as did Jacques, helping the group forward.

Bart was screaming to Ahiga: *"FORZA, AHIGA, FORZA AMICO!"* The Italian didn't like to even get scratched but he took out one of the defensemen as well. It was not one of favorite pastimes but it was a necessity he gladly endured, even though he got banged up doing it.

"Ahiga's on their thirty-yard line, now the twenty!" Tony was shouting enthusiastically in his microphone.

The entire Natives' staff, players who were not on the field, as well as Oliver and Maxine were running down the sideline as if in slow motion, cheering their team on. They were all going about the same speed.

Both teams were now surrounding the ball carrier. The

Natives were just not going to let their rivals get that ball, but one of them jumped through the wall of bodies and tried to reach it. Ahiga saw him out of the corner of his eye and tossed the ball back to Neil who had caught up with the group and was running right behind them. The quarterback wasn't expecting that, but he was a quick thinker and yelled out: "I've got it, but keep running, Ahiga, stay with me, stay right behind me!" Neil ran in front of his buddy. Ahiga nodded and did as Neil said.

"What was that?" Tony asked.

"He passed it back to Neil and now he's in front of that human carousel," Laura answered excitedly, yet just as bewildered.

They all kept running, offense protecting, defense bouncing off the Natives. Zorba threw himself at an opposing player's legs who went down. The Samoan Vaimoas were doing shades of *deashi*, the sumo constant forward movement while jogging. It really couldn't quite be called running. Toma held his left arm out, firm as a steel rod. Ualesi held his arms close to his brothers, and Viliamu held his right arm out as if it was Hercules' shield. They made sure their arms were as solid as a jouster's lance.

"They're on the ten! They're on the five! They're almost there..." Tony was yelling into the mic.

"The big boys are going to do it! Between the Sumos and Ahiga they are pounding the ground with at least a half a ton! I bet the earth is shaking!" Laura screamed as well.

"I don't know about the earth, but the stands sure are!"

The spectators were on a crazy high. They shouted and supported their team. They also stomped their feet to the feverish beat of the drums.

William Quinn, Uncle Frank, Roberta and Charles, the mayor of Albuquerque, celebrities and prominent members of the Natives' entourage were on their feet, their hands on the glass in front of them as they watched from the V.I.P. boxes. They screamed just as loud as the fans in the bleachers. The drummers in the stands were banging on the skins to the rhythm of Ahiga's steps. Every time one of his feet touched the grass, they would bang the drums. The fans joined in with GO, GO, GO on each of the drummers' hits.

The Vaimoas brothers were still preventing the defensive players to get to Neil, who knew the clock had run out. He slowed his pace so that the wrestlers and Ahiga could keep up. Hopefully they would be able to make it all the way into the end zone and score that coveted touchdown. The pace was so slow that the fallen players actually got up and tried to reach the little carousel. The Natives didn't stop either. They either followed their opponents or surrounded their teammates running with the ball. Suddenly Neil turned around and, still running, backwards this time looked at Ahiga. "Catch the ball!" Neil yelled and tossed it to his spiritual buddy. The Navajo man was surprised but he caught the ball easily with his large hands and followed the quarterback's direction. "Now follow me! Take it in, big boy!" He shouted.

"What was that?" Tony asked, for the hundredth time.

"I think he wants a true local Native to score the championship touchdown," Laura answered her partner.

Just a few feet more. It was coming up on them: The end zone, the zero-yard line, the goal line.

"The defense can't stop them!" Tony hollered.

"They're going to make it!" Laura screamed.

"He's going to score! The big man is going to score!"

"The biggest and slowest guys on the team ran all the way from the ten-yard line! Are you kidding me?" Laura exclaimed. "When's the last time you saw a Center score a touchdown?"

"And they're still going! Must have been the drumming from the fans pushing them on. They have been relentless!"

"And I would venture to say very helpful."

The entire Natives' offense crossed that final line with the ball in Ahiga's hand high above his head and scored the game's winning touchdown.

The tallest man on the team stood in the middle of the end zone holding the ball in the air. The Sumos fell on the grass exhausted and lay there like cats sleeping on their backs with their paws to their sides.

"*Shini-tai*," Tomo said breathlessly.

His brothers laughed.

"Hey, T.," Neil said looking down at his teammate. What does shini-tai mean?"

"It's a sumo term. Literally it means dead body," Ualesi said

"Oh, dude, I like that!" Neil chuckled, "but I think we did a shini-tai on the other team."

The triplets nodded and gave him a thumbs up. Their brief relaxation didn't last long as the rest of the team jumped all over them. Zorba had to use some gymnastics skills to jump up to Ahiga's neck. The tall man knew he wouldn't be able to stay upright for long. He finally crumbled under most of his team, but he didn't mind, it was worth it. They became a pile of dark orange and tan bodies, one on top of the other, screaming and shouting with complete joy. Ahiga closed his eyes for a moment and said a silent prayer to his Spirits. They finally stood up and this winning team helped the big boys up. They huddled, put their hands together and shouted "HONEEZNÁ! WIN! *We won!* We are New Mexico Natives football! We are from the Land of Enchantment! We are Enchanted Football!"

They quickly formed a circle and started dancing the Native American steps. The mascot joined them, as did everyone from the sideline who had been running along. The spectators in the stands and in the VIP booths did the steps as well. It was a glorious Pow Wow as players, spectators and staff danced and chanted in the bleachers and on the field. In the stands the drumming and chanting was louder than it had ever been. Some of the players rushed to Oliver and Maxine and started throwing them in the air. George tried to disappear but others caught up with him and he too became a human ball.

The press was having a field day, literally. The reporters and cameramen were all present on the grass. They were projecting the historical events unfolding before them and the jumbotron seemed looped to the last winning play.

"What a brilliant performance! A well-oiled machine. Bravo!" Tony exclaimed.

"Truly! They deserved to win. That was amazing and pretty damn unique! And would you check out the coaches being tossed up and down," Laura laughed.

"I guess they either forgot the Gatorade shower or just preferred to toss their coaches like a salad.

The stage for the trophy presentations was quickly set up and several football executives walked up the stairs to the platform. Among them were William Quinn, Oliver Hadley, Neil Howard, and the NFL commissioner.

The first trophy was the MVP and was handed to Neil Howard. The crowd cheered. They had followed the man's career and were glad he was back. The quarterback brought the trophy to his lips and kissed it. In a split-second his mind replayed the events of the last few months: The escape from the loan sharks, his first meeting with Coach Hadley, the suffocation in front of the casino, the sweat lodge with Ahiga, the tough practices, his leadership with his players and the games. The culmination was the success of this day. He went up to Oliver and hugged the man he loved, the one who believed in him, the one who had given him a second chance at a career and at life. Neil Howard was on top of the world and wanted to make sure his coach knew that it was thanks to him. The hug between the two men made it perfectly clear. When they came apart no words were needed and Oliver just winked at him. Neil nodded back.

"Well, the New England Patriots have Belichick and Brady, but the Natives have Howard and Hadley," Laura said from the announcers' booth.

"This might be the next great football duo," Tony added.

"And to think that the man no one thought would last more than a couple of weeks, let alone the whole season, wound up as the MVP and a Champ," Laura said.

"It's all in believing in second chances. Bravo to Coach Hadley."

"Yes, well done indeed, to both of them."

Neil was handed a microphone. He held his award in one hand and with his other brought the mic in front of his face and started talking. The crowd listened.

"I was born twice, first by the best parents in the world and then again by Coach Hadley. He brought me out of a dark abyss, more than once, and gave me a second chance. I am the luckiest man alive and extremely grateful to everyone in the organization, especially Coach

Hadley and Mr. Quinn. And a special thanks to Ahiga. The team, nor I, wouldn't be the same without you. You are our center." Neil was thinking of the first time they met and wound up in the sweat lodge. "No man has ever had as beautiful family as I have! Look at them!" Neil hollered and gestured to all the players from his team standing in front of the stage. He kissed the trophy and lifted it high above his head. "We did it!"

The players and the fans screamed in delight and respect.

The next trophy was the coveted Vince Lombardi trophy and it was being carried toward the platform. A Hall of Famer, a man who had been one of the great football players and now a legend, was walking with it through the 'alley' of New Mexico Natives players where each one either touched or kissed the silver statue. As excited as they were, they stood respectfully as it passed them. They were humbled by the award, by their achievement and by the history they helped create. It was a boyhood dream they had all had, and now as young men it was a moment of accomplishment in their lives they would never forget. The Hall of Famer continued on and up to the platform where he handed the trophy over to the commissioner of the NFL, who in turn said a few congratulatory words to William and presented him with the award his team had won. The owner lifted it up to all to see—the fans, the players and the staff. The confetti poured down continuously over everyone present in the stadium.

William took the microphone handed to him and looked at the sea of people in front and all around him. "People ask me 'what do you think is the reason for your success?' My answer is: It is everyone involved with the New Mexico Natives, including the fans!" The crowd roared. "But if I could pinpoint the reason I would say: Oliver Hadley." More cheering from the fans and from the players. "The man is the best coach in the world, a leader, a gentleman and a man I am proud to have known for almost twenty years. To me he is also a friend and brother. What he and his staff have accomplished is simply amazing and pure finesse. His success is measured not only with talent but with heart. I would wish every person could have the good fortune of having an Oliver Hadley in their lives." He gave Oliver an enormous hug and gave him the microphone.

"Thanks, Will. You move mountains, my friend. You had a dream and you wanted me to be part of it. I thought you were crazy!" The crowd laughed along with him. "But I should have known better. You are a unique human being with more heart and energy than anyone can measure. Thank you, Will, for this amazing opportunity and for being in my life." The two old friends hugged each other again. Oliver looked at the crowd and said: "The man is already talking about next season!" The audience roared and clapped again. It also gave them an anticipated thrill of a new season. Oliver continued. "Winning such an award is not about one, two, or a few people, but by everyone on a team! No coach could be more proud of each and every player and staff member who is part of the New Mexico Natives. Every single one contributed blood, sweat and tears, in addition to hours of dedication and love for their trade. Most of all they shared their hearts. The trophy could not have been won without each and every member of the Natives, and that includes the fans!" Oliver raised the trophy into the air and shouted: "We will never forget this season!" The drums reverberated and the crowd cheered.

From the announcers booth Tony and Laura were

quiet as they listened to the speeches. When they were over Tony spoke into his mic: "I must say those were pretty nice speeches."

"I agree with you, Tony. Very well said indeed. And as Hadley mentioned they're already thinking about next season. I'm so glad the Natives stayed alive. We were all wondering what would happen after that dreadful accident," Laura added.

"World champions have stood on that platform and made history, either as an owner, a coach or a player, and tonight is no exception. William Quinn, Oliver Hadley, Neil Howard, along with their staff and players are the first team to win the trophy in their entry year. No one else has ever done that, no Native American has ever carried the ball for the winning touchdown of the biggest game of the season. And definitely no new football team has lost so many players because of a terrible accident."

"Thankfully they will all recover. And what a comeback for a team. These guys are amazing. This definitely is one to remember!"

"Yes, bravo to the New Mexico Natives. Really well done. Thank you for such an enlightening season. We'll see you in a few months. In the meantime I'm Tony Schuster with my colleague Laura Sullivan." Tony turned and looked at his younger colleague and said to her: "Laura, it has been a privilege working with you this historic season. Today was special and I thank you for being my colleague, not just today but since we started together. All broadcasters should be as lucky as I am. Your father would have been proud of you."

Laura immediately hugged him. "Thank you, Tony. I couldn't have asked for a more special person to work with. Not only are you the epitome of a great broadcaster but also incredibly knowledgeable and have the biggest heart in the world. *I'm* the lucky one. I hope we will be doing this together for a long time."

"I wish the same thing, young lady." Tony took a quick, deep breath. He realized how much he loved the young woman and immediately thought of his daughter and all the girls who followed Laura. She was an inspiration and he was grateful she was in all their lives. He once again spoke into the microphone: "Ladies and gentlemen, thank you for having been with us. We hope you enjoyed the season, and especially today's big game. Until we are together again, we wish you goodnight."

"Goodnight, everybody," Laura concluded.

CHAPTER 26   THE FIESTA

Albuquerque's mayor announced a holiday—'New Mexico Natives' day—a day where schools would be closed and a parade would be held in honor of the recently crowned champions. The celebration would be held at Balloon Fiesta Park to commemorate the historic achievement.

The Albuquerque park was home to several annual events, the greatest being the most photographed event in the world, the Albuquerque International Balloon Fiesta, which annually hosted almost a million people and over five hundred hot air balloons with their pilots and crews. The park was enormous at seventy-eight acres, and when those iridescent hot air balloons ascended into the unique New Mexico sky it became a canvas of floating Christmas ornaments. On this day, however, the area measuring fifty-four football fields would be hosting a parade for the champions from the Land of Enchantment. It was the best place in the city to hold the venue, with ample parking, a huge area for the parade and the fans, and of course many stands and food trucks with beverages and food.

The majority of the field was set up like a street, with police barricades along the sides. The fans were lined up behind them and when the open-air buses carrying the

New Mexico Natives team drove along the route in front of them, they screamed and shouted enthusiastically. The vehicles were decorated with the team colors and logos on the banners hanging down the sides. The players wore their jerseys with their numbers and many in the crowd wore them as well. One of the buses carried William, Oliver, Maxine, Dezba and the rest of the staff including George and Isaac. Among them were the mayor of the city, the University president of UNM and their entourages. On another bus the *unconventionals* were the fan favorites. They waved to the crowd and Neil and Ahiga held the trophy together and showed it off. At the same time several jumbotrons around the field projected shots of the people in the buses and faces in the crowd surrounding them. Interspersed were highpoints from the Natives' games including Ahiga's winning touchdown, the Vaimoa triplets' 'wall', and Bart's bicycle kick among many other highlights.

Leaders, dancers, singers and drummers from the nineteen pueblos and three reservations of New Mexico were present as well and showed off their unique and stunning outfits while dancing and drumming. They, too, were projected on the big screens. The fans heartily clapped and praised everyone incessantly.

There was also a stage set up and when the Natives ended the drive, they left the buses and sat on the bleachers reserved for them next to the stage. The injured players were among the champions. Some were in wheelchairs and casts and all were present sporting championship jerseys. Thankfully not one of the players had lost their life. Most would soon be able to play again. Everyone in the Natives organization had gone to visit each and every one of them when they had been laid up. William even more so. He found out details about their families and their dreams. He helped as much as he could. He went to see them all the time and provided the men with every kind of support they needed. If they were unable to continue playing football, William made sure they would be able to excel in another field they were interested in. If they needed schooling to pursue a dream he provided that as well.

Being in Albuquerque, and especially at Balloon Fiesta Park, there were, of course, several hot air balloons, and they slowly descended in designated areas in the corners of the park. It was especially impressive as dusk was turning into night and when the pilots directed fire into their envelopes, they glowed bright and beautiful. Several represented the New Mexico symbol, the Zia, on the sides of their inflated envelopes. There were others, such as a football and another a map of the world. The impressive pilots landed the giants smoothly and gently and kept the envelope inflated as their crews tethered them in place.

"You can thank the Montgolfier brothers for the hot air balloons. They were French of course and made the first ones," Jacques said with pride.

"Yes, but don't forget about Icarus," the Greek man responded immediately, "*we* were the first to fly."

Jacques laughed. "But look what happened to him. He didn't pay attention to his *Papa* and flew too close to the sun and *au-revoir*, bye-bye, his wings melted."

"Ah, that doesn't matter," Zorba said.

The two close buddies bickered on good naturedly for quite a while. By the time they finished they probably would have either resolved world hunger or created a way to fly to the stars, without wax on their wings of course. Sitting next to them were Delmar, waving to all the ladies in the crowd; Bartolomeo who followed suit, and the

Vaimoa triplets who had become darlings of the fans as well.

Several people on the stage were sitting in chairs. Among them were William, Oliver, Maxine and Dezba. Neil was there as the recipient of the MVP award. Ahiga and Bart were also present, as was an older man in his nineties. He wore a yellow shirt, a red vest and red garrison cap adorned with several pins, including the Marine Corps logo. Around his neck a chain of turquoise and silver hung majestically and complimented the impressive military ribbons marking his service as a Code Talker during WWII in the battle of the Pacific.

The mayor was speaking into a microphone giving a speech, praising the Natives for their accomplishment and to the organization for giving Albuquerque and the state recognition and financial benefits. He finished by announcing that two additional and new trophies, ones specifically designed for players on the Natives' team. They were the Jim Thorpe trophy and the Navajo Code Talkers trophy and would be given to exceptional players. The Lombardi stood majestically on a table in front of them. William said a few congratulatory words and presented the Jim Thorpe trophy to Bart as the most inspirational player. Bartolomeo Bacci bowed deeply and shook William's hand. He took the trophy, kissed it and raised it above his head for all to see. He left the stage and went to sit with his teammates.

William had invited Tony and Laura who happily accepted and were broadcasting again.

"That's a nice trophy and Kisses definitely deserves it," Tony said.

"Yeah, the man sure had some creative moves."

"True, and look where those moves got him. And let's not forget Zorba's Mary Lou and one of the sumos lifting the pants right up that player?"

"How could I forget?"

The next trophy, the Navajo Code Talkers trophy, was presented by the Code Talker to the player who was a pillar of the team and most enlightened others. The old, noble Marine proudly handed it over to Ahiga. The big man accepted it graciously, made a fist with his right hand and put it over his heart, a sign of thanks for the courage.

"Well, that was pretty perfect. The big Navajo was definitely the right choice," Tony said.

"Agreed."

The players on the Natives team also agreed. They genuinely loved Ahiga and thought maybe the sage's smoke, as well as the big man's Spirits, had helped.

Neil handed a microphone to Ahiga and hugged him. "I love you, man," he whispered in the big man's ear. Ahiga winked back at him. He then closed his eyes. He didn't say anything and the crowd quieted down as they wondered what he was up to. He seemed to be meditating. He slowly opened his eyes and then quickly raised the trophy above his head. "HONEEZNÁ! WE WIN!" Ahiga shouted. The crowd answered back just as enthusiastically. He put the microphone close to his face. "We made history because we are one. We have come from the earth of the Land of Enchantment, or from faraway lands in the middle of oceans or from a different continent. We are of all nationalities, of all colors, of different religions, we are each one of us unique but all the same. Together we win! "HONEEZNÁ! The big man bowed his head, handed over the microphone to William and left the stage. The crowd clapped enthusiastically and as after each speech the drums resonated. He called Oliver up to him and then turned to the crowd.

"Ladies and gentlemen, this man, Oliver Hadley, is the main reason for the Natives' success. Not only is he the best coach in the world..." the fans interrupted to clap profusely. They loved Oliver as well. William continued: "I am also fortunate to call him my best friend. He is like a brother." The crowd clapped some more. He turned to Oliver and said: "I need you for one more thing."

"What do you need?" Oliver asked.

"Make sure I don't fall." It was a strange statement coming from William but Oliver knew what he was up to. William extended his arm toward Dezba. She took his hand and he lifted her to her feet. He kissed her hand, smiled at her and got down on one knee. The spectators gasped, some stifled screams. Dezba was just as surprised, but she knew William truly loved her as she loved him. There was no doubt they wanted to spend their lives together. William pulled a ring out of his pocket and asked her to marry him in front of the world.

The spectators strained to hear Dezba's answer.

"Yes," she whispered.

"Louder!" Someone shouted from the crowd.

Everybody laughed and Dezba obliged them. "Yes! Yes! Yes!" She shouted with glee.

William and Dezba kissed, to the delight of the fans.

The spectators had not expected this addition to the day's events.

"Hey, Oliver, would you be my best man?" William asked.

"Absolutely, under one condition," he answered.

The crowd was now part of the show and they wanted to know what the condition was.

"What condition?" William asked.

Oliver stood up from his chair, took Maxine's hand and as William had with Dezba, got down on one knee and produced a ring.

The crowd went crazy and screamed. Another proposal!

"Lady Maxine Owen-Smith, would you do me the great honor of being my wife?" Oliver asked.

The smile was the most radiant from any woman's lips Oliver had ever seen. He would make it his life's mission to make that smile appear on her lovely face every day of their lives.

"It would be my pleasure, my lord," she said and kissed him.

The fans went wild. Engagements were always fun and tear-jerkers, but this one took the cake! There wasn't a dry eye at the park as everyone witnessed the proposals on the stage in front of them or on the jumbotrons. The women were all wiping tears from their cheeks and quite a few guys had wet eyes. They were happy for the two men who had brought them the Natives team. They loved and respected them and were now ecstatic for their happiness.

Oliver and William looked at each other and shouted at the same time: "HONEEZNÁ! We won!"

The fans followed suit and cheered with them to the sounds of drums and singing from the loudspeakers throughout the field.

"Oh, my," Laura said. "I didn't think the Natives could surprise us any more than they already had."

"New Mexico Natives. That's all you need to know," Tony said.

William and Oliver looked at the crowd, took each other's hands and bowed to their devotees. They gave each other a hug and then went to their new fiancées and grabbed them and hugged all together.

The crowd was just as ecstatic, with the engagements, with the trophy and with their historic achievement. It was a season to remember.

EPILOGUE  THE NEXT IDEA?

The engaged couples were enjoying a quiet moment with a Cognac in William's penthouse. They warmed the amber liquid with their hands and sipped the brandy. The lights of the city winked at them as if thanking them for the season and for the amazing events that took place that day at the Balloon Fiesta Park. The couples looked at each other and smiled.

"This has been the most exciting year of my life," Dezba said.

"I couldn't agree with you more," Maxine added.

"We started this just a year ago, Will," Oliver said to his long-time friend.

They stared at the trophy standing on a table.

"It is beautiful," Dezba said respectfully.

"The Vince Lombardi Trophy is twenty-two inches tall, weighs seven pounds and is entirely made of sterling silver," William volunteered. The man knew something about jewelry and precious metals.

"A nice little bauble for your trophy case," Oliver said, slapping his best buddy on the back.

"It is magnificent, and the *Natives'* trophy case is going to be a big one with I'm sure, many, many awards decorating it."

"You think so?" Oliver asked.

"Only with you at the head of it. What do you say?"

"I have Native blood in my veins."

"You do?"

"In one way or another," Oliver grinned.

"Ladies?" William asked.

"Absolutely," Dezba answered.

"I'm in too," Maxine said.

William stared in front of him as if he were watching an invisible film being projected inside his mind just behind his forehead.

"Earth to William," Oliver sing-songed as he snapped his fingers, "where are you?"

Maxine, Dezba and Oliver recognized the glow in Williams's eyes. The man was planning something. He was in that state of trance. His gaze was fixed, yet unfocused. His mind, however, was definitely tuned in to this new idea brewing.

"Oh, oh," Maxine said. "Oh, William, great wise chief, hellooooo."

"Will's a great wise chief?" Oliver asked.

"That's what the name William means."

"Of course, appropriate," Oliver groaned.

"Will, what are you concocting now?" Dezba asked.

"He's figuring out the most original place for a honeymoon," Oliver said.

"That sounds nice," Dezba said.

Will came out of his reverie. "I have a question for all you, tell me which you prefer: New Mexico Nativettes or Lady Natives?"

Oh, no! Oliver's mind screamed. His eyes grew wide and he shook his head. Then he started laughing as he knew William was joking. Or was he?

About the Author

My very first memory of life was the sound of my mother's glorious voice singing to me, most likely a Brahms lullaby. I'm convinced that is why music always has a delicious way of creeping into my writing and becomes an integral part of my novels. I lived in Europe for over twenty years while my father was a diplomat with the U.S. State Department. This provided the basis for many of my story themes and settings, and my love for languages, five of which I speak fluently and use quite often when recording audiobooks (my own as well as other authors').

I write different genres: Romance, Adventure, Metaphysical, Military and Historical fiction. My non-fiction work includes a photo book, 'Around the World in 80 Quotes on Photos', and 'Travel Tales', short adventure stories from different places around the globe. 'Violet's Voyages', is a Children's Books series I created for my granddaughter.
I believe there is no stronger bond than sharing a book. My desire is that my work entertains and informs, and that my readers, from 3 to 103 years young, cherish the time reading and discovering together.

I am a proud mother of a gallant Marine Veteran, and among the members of our household you will find Louie the cat (aka King Louie XIX), so named because of his clawing love of Louis XV and XVI furniture, and surely thinks he was a king in one of his former lives.

Acknowledgments

Pamela Carter, Georgia and Barry Sigmon, thank you for your wonderful friendship and for all the gracious help and suggestions with this novel.

A Note from the Author

On my website you will find photos and music featured around the characters and locations in 'Enchanted Football' (and my other books as well). Please enjoy.

denisekahnbooks.com/photomusic-gallery/

If you would like information on new releases and events make sure you sign up for my newsletter.
You will automatically receive a **FREE** PDF of 'Around the World in 80 Quotes on Photos'.

DeniseKahnBooks.com

I love hearing from my readers and I answer all my mail personally. Thank you for your interest and for reading!

e-mail: Denise@DeniseKahnBooks.com

Denise's books

Peace of Music

A once lost magnificent antique vase from China's 13th Century Song Dynasty reappears from the depths of the Mediterranean Sea where it comes to dwell on a piano in a doctor's home. It becomes the impetus in steering the lives of this doctor and his descendants through their heartbreaks, romances and ultimately successes. An assassination, a sabotage on a Greek island and amazing musical performances are but some of the events that strike their lives. Spanning from 13th Century China to the present, the story takes place on four continents, with talented individuals of different nationalities and backgrounds, always interrelated by music.

Obsession of the Heart

Set against an international backdrop of jet setters, music, romance, murder, terrorism and true friendship is Davina Walters, an international singer. Davina meets Jean, a young woman almost paralyzed with fear, as her sadistic ex-husband is bent on killing her. On the spur of the moment Davina decides to take her along on tour and the murderer plans his ultimate revenge in a deadly showdown.

Warrior Music

Max knew the drugs and alcohol would eventually kill him, and sooner rather than later. So he enlisted in the Marines. His timing is unfortunate, as the events of 9/11 find him at the beginning of his military service, and he is sent to Iraq. The journey he embarks on is unlike anything he could ever imagine.
From Washington, Boston and New Orleans to the ancient sands of Iraq, Max and his entourage endure the toils of war with gallantry, patriotism, courage, heartache and passion.
Only one weapon gets them through the anguish they come face to face with... Music.

The Music Trilogy

The Music Trilogy, a family saga, is a compilation of three books: *Peace of Music, Obsession of the Heart* and *Warrior Music*, a combination of historical fiction, thriller, romance, military prowess and music—something for every taste. The Music Trilogy can be read or listened to in sequence or each book as a stand-alone.

Split-Second Lifetime

On a business trip from the U.S. to Paris, Jebby meets Dodi on a flight. Jebby is an ethnomusicologist, and Dodi is an international photographer. They are immediately attracted to each other, but from the very first moment Dodi triggers what seems like past life memories for Jebby of a poignant and passionate time they shared together. As Jebby tries to figure out if she is "losing it" or if past lives really do exist, they embark on a path of adventure and romance where lifetimes and cultures interweave in modern day Paris, Uzbekistan, and in the old Southwest. Jebby and Dodi live their unusually diverse and rich adventure and romance, surrounded by an international cast and superb musicians. At the same time Jebby discovers where the Hopi originated from, that death is not a finality, love transcends lifetimes, and music is eternal.

Hot Air

A thriller filled with passion, romance, survival and courage. Sean Sandoval, half Navajo, half Irish, has bravery in his blood and passion in his heart. From boyhood to one of the Air Force's elite Pararescuemen, his path in life is always connected to air. As a hot air balloon pilot Sean communes with that air. As a Pararescuer he flies into danger to saves lives.
An enemy combatant from the mountains of Afghanistan, presumed killed, arrives in Albuquerque, New Mexico and is bent on such revenge that he puts thousands of people at the annual International Balloon Fiesta in lethal danger. Will Sean stop him in time?

Guitar Woman (novella)

Filled with romance, suspense, passion, and set in beautiful Greek locations.

Alex Kouros's passions are making exquisite guitars and producing Greece's premier beer. At a prestigious art gallery he meets artist Cassandra Beckham. A whirlwind romance ensues, but is cut short when malicious kidnappers board the yacht they are sailing on in the turquoise waters of the Aegean. As they struggle with the malefactors Alex is shot and Cassie falls into the sea with a blow to her head. They are left for dead, and although they survive they both think the other died.

Alex blames himself and tries to drown his sorrows with his brew. Cassie washes up on a deserted beach of a tiny island.
Will they be destined to find each other again?

Around the World in 80 Quotes on Photos

A photograph portrays a thousand words. A quote is but a few more powerful ones. Together they are food for the senses. They make us think, wonder, and engulf us. They represent traditions, civilizations, cultures, and offer us splendor, progress, grand vistas and minute details, all in a planet rich in majestic beauty. Embark on this journey of quotes and photographs, from ancient sands to calm seas, from sky to pebbles, from natural magnificence to man-made luxury.
Photographs were taken in countries around the world.

Travel Tales

Travel Tales is a series of short travel stories, journeys spiced with humor and interesting international characters in famous or little known places.
True stories of the author finding herself in adventures in foreign lands while discovering different cultures, local folklore, food, music, and sometimes danger.

We were 12 at 12:12 on 12/12/12 (Mexico)
Entertained by the Gods (Greece)
Sai Baba's Ashram Rendezvous (India)
Gstaad Grace (Switzerland)
Thanksgiving in 24 Hours (Mexico)
Olympic Honor (Italy)

Violet's Voyages
(Children's Series)
Switzerland: The St. Bernard Adventure

All novels available as e-books and audiobooks.

For more information please visit:
DeniseKahnBooks.com   /   DeniseKahnVoices.com

www.ingramcontent.com/pod-product-compliance
Lightning Source LLC
Chambersburg PA
CBHW021647110726

47902CB00007B/1866